I0524203

Swordsman Of the Rift

Bra...

Artist
Lonwa A

SWORDSMAN OF THE RIFT

Volume 6

Written by Brandon Varnell
Illustrations by Lonwa_A

This book is a work of fiction. Names, characters, places, and incidents are the products of the author's imagination or are used fictitiously. Any resemblance to actual events, locales, or persons, living or dead, is coincidental.

Swordsman of the Rift
Copyright © 2019 Brandon Varnell
Illustration Copyright © 2019 Lonwa_A
All rights reserved.

To see Brandon Varnell's other works, or to ask for permission to use his works, visit him at www.varnell-brandon.com, facebook at www.facebook.com/AmericanKitsune, twitter at www.twitter.com/BrandonbVarnell, Patreon at https://www.patreon.com/BrandonVarnell, and instagram at www.instagram.com/brandonbvarnell.

ISBN: 978-0-9989942-8-4

CONTENT

CHAPTER 1

Blood stained my body. Screams of terror echoed in my ears. A world of fire and death and flying body parts filled my vision. I saw people dying left and right, mowed down by gunfire, soaring through the air as they were hit with explosions. Heat seared my skin and shockwaves rattled my brain and bones.

"CHRIS!!!"

A shout erupted from my mouth as my best friend's lifeless corpse hit the ground beside me, his body half burnt to a crisp, eyelids melted off, revealing glazed-over eye sockets, and a pool of blood spreading out beneath him. Pain ripped through me as I opened my mouth again to scream…

And then I opened my eyes and found a ceiling above me. I blinked once, twice, and then relaxed as the softness of the bed and the warm, very feminine body resting against me, made me realize where I was. This was not the battlefield. There was no war. There was just me, the woman beside me, and this bed.

I still felt a little sick.

Climbing to my feet as I removed the woman's limbs from around my body, I stumbled around the completely unfamiliar bedroom. Soft carpet stretched out beneath my feet. I glanced at the large dresser to one side, sitting next to a sliding door that probably led to a closet space. When I turned around, I noticed the massive window dominating one side of the room. From the view I could, I could tell this was a penthouse.

I found a door several yards to my left and walked through it. A relieved sigh escaped my lips when I realized this was a restroom. Tiled floor. Marble countertop. Sink. Toilet. The whole shebang. I noticed there was no shower, but I spotted a door at the other end, so I assumed the shower and the toilet were separated.

Walking up to the sink, I placed my hand over the sensor bar, which turned on the hot water. I splashed the water on my face, then placed my hands against the counter and took several deep breaths.

Another dream. Another nightmare.

I wondered when they would end, but it had been two years since my military service ended, and I was still having nightmares of the things I'd seen.

Looking up, I stared at my reflection in the mirror. My pale skin was marked by a cross-shaped scar on my left cheek. Pale blue eyes gazed at me from beneath my eyebrows. My eyes were a little sunken in, my face a little hollow, but I was clean shaven at least. A head of messy light-brown hair sat on my head. Someone once told me I looked like Ryan Reynolds with my current haircut. It was such a great compliment I decided to keep my hair like this.

I also hadn't lost my physique, which I'd earned from my time in the military. Broad chest and shoulders, powerful abs and legs, the V-shaped cut a lot of bodybuilders tried to attain. If nothing else, I should probably be proud of myself for keeping up my exercise regimen even though I was no longer in the military.

As I stood there, a loud beeping went off in the bedroom. It took me a second to recognize the ringing of my phone. Walking back into the bedroom, I saw the blonde woman shifted in bed.

"What is that... noise?" she asked.

"Just my phone, babe. Don't mind it. You can go back to sleep," I said.

The woman shifted against the covers again, burying her head into the pillow as I grabbed my phone and went through a door that led into an expensively furnished living room. I didn't pay attention to the furnishings much as I looked at the Caller ID.

Elric Fuller.

I frowned, but then shook my head and accepted the call.

"Elric?" I said.

"Hey, Bryan. It's been awhile, hasn't it?" a familiar voice came from the other end.

"It has been a long time since we last talked. About a year, if I'm not mistaken." I paused. "What do you want?"

"What's this? Why do you suspect I want something? Can't a man call his friend every so often to see how he's doing?"

"There's nothing wrong with that, but we both know you never call someone just to 'see how they're doing.' You only ever call when you want something." I wandered over to the wall and leaned against it. The coolness of the wall felt great against my back. "So spill. What's so important that you'd call me up? What do you want?"

"Okay. You got me. I do have something I want." Elric paused for effect, but I just sighed. *"So, I know this guy who has a job lined up for me. A huge gig that pays good money. He's getting together a team. Says he wants people with combat experience, so I forwarded your name to him. I was thinking you could do this as a distraction. You haven't been doing well since your service ended, right? He's interested and wants to know if you'd like the job."*

I frowned. I wasn't really looking for a job, and Elric knew that, but he also knew I probably needed something to distract myself. He was right. I hadn't been doing well since my service ended—no, I'd probably been in this state since before my service ended, if I was being honest.

I took in the room as I thought. It really was a nice room. Spacious, with an entertainment area embedded a few feet below that could be accessed via a short staircase. The furnishings were all nice, beautifully hand-crafted items made from leather and natural wood. I didn't want to know how much this furniture and that brand new holographic projector cost.

"Tell him... I'm interested," I said at last.

"You can tell him yourself. We're meeting tonight. I'll forward you the address."

"Yeah. Sure. That's fine."

Once he had confirmation that I was in, Elric hung up. I received an email seconds later. A glance at my inbox said I had one new message from Elric Fuller. When I opened it, I saw that he'd uploaded a detailed map of where I was supposed to meet. As if gravity was affecting my mouth, my lips turned into a frown when I noticed the meeting was to take place in an abandoned warehouse. That seemed pretty shady. However, Elric knew I'd never do something that was illegal, so this gig should be on the up and up.

I glanced back into the bedroom. The woman still lay sleeping on the bed. I didn't know her name, what she did for a living, or anything about her. We'd met in a bar last night. She complained about her ex-husband, the struggles of her divorce, and I merely listened because I didn't have anything better to do at the time. Then she asked me to come over.

I didn't have a reason to say no.

After spending another moment looking at her, I wandered into the kitchen and decided to make the woman breakfast. It was the least I could do for showing me a good time last night. She'd want something nice and greasy anyway. Given how much she drank, she was bound to have a hangover.

***

There were a lot of abandoned warehouses on the south side of the city. These large buildings, no longer working or running, looked like they might be haunted.

I found Elric standing outside the warehouse on my map. He was a tall man at about two heads taller than myself, putting him at a good 6'7" or so. His blond hair was immaculately combed to one side. Bright blue eyes, a trimmed beard, and a physique similar to my own gave him the look of a standard pretty boy, the kind who could make their entire living by seducing women. He was wearing black pants, a black shirt, and an overcoat. White breath steamed from his mouth as he broke out in a smile.

"Bryan, good of you to make it," he said, clasping my hand in a firm shake.

It was a cold night. My body was covered in goosebumps as I wore the same thing I'd been wearing at the bar last night. I wasn't dressed for the cold like Elric was. However, the cold was never something that bothered me.

"What's this job your friend has lined up?" I asked.

"All in good time, my man," Elric said as he slung an arm around my shoulder and led me toward a door located just beside the warehouse's main entrance. "For now, let me introduce you to the team we're working with."

We walked through a hall before entering another door, which led into the warehouse itself. This place was mostly empty. Aside from the girders, stairs, and unused power equipment, the only other thing inside were a group of people and several objects that looked like incredibly high-tech and sophisticated recliners.

As we walked forward, the people turned to study us, and I in turn studied them. There were three others aside from Elric and me. Two women and one man.

The man was another one of those pretty boys. His dark hair was meticulously combed. He was in good physical shape, though I could tell it was the kind you got from going to the gym.

The two women looked like they were also in good shape. One of them actually had bigger muscles than the man. She was tall, had dark skin and broad shoulders. She wore an outfit that vaguely resembled army fatigues, which went nicely with her short hair. Meanwhile, the other girl was far more petite, but she had slender shoulders, a thin waist, and skinny arms and legs. Actually, now that I was looking at her, I could tell that she was just skinny and not in good physical shape. Her physique made me think of people who sat behind a desk all day. She had light skin that was almost porcelain, dark hair that seemed black, and even darker eyes. Judging from the shape of her face, I could tell she was Asian or of Asian descent.

"Bryan, that guy right there is Brad. He's the one putting all this together. The dark-skinned gal over there is Vyra, and the little Chinese lady is Ju Chen." He introduced each person in turn, then unslung his arm from around my shoulder and pointed at me. "Everyone, this is Bryan Jenson."

"I've heard of you," the dark-skinned woman, Vyra, said. Her eyes narrowed. "You're the one they called Invincible back when I was in the Marines. Rumor has it you're the youngest member to ever join the Special Forces, and you've completed more missions than any Marine alive today."

I grimaced when I heard the words. So this woman was ex-military too? That might make things unpleasant for me, as I'd been doing my best to avoid anything that had to do with the military. Even so, I tried not to let my reticence show on my face.

"I'm surprised people still talk about me," I said, shrugging.

"They might not anymore. I got out of the Marines about a year ago." Vyra shrugged, then looked me over once more, from my head to my toes. "Somehow, I expected you to be... I don't know, a bit more dangerous-looking, I guess."

"Sorry to disappoint." I shrugged. It didn't matter to me what preconceived notions about myself I shattered. "So, can I know what we're going now?" I turned to the one called Brad, even as I hooked a thumb at Elric. "This guy wouldn't tell me a single thing."

"Don't look at me." Elric held his hands up in a helpless gesture. "I don't know anymore than I already told you."

Brad nodded and smiled. "Now that we're all here, I'll be more than happy to let you know what we're doing."

He walked over to the recliners, which I now realized had what appeared to be an advanced vitals monitoring system attached to each one. A holographic monitoring function hovered over them. It was currently blank. What caught my attention even more were the objects sitting on each recliner. It looked like a black full-bodysuit and a sleek helmet.

"I'm sure all of you have heard about VR technology these days," Brad began as he patted one of the recliners. "It's pretty much everywhere these days. Shops, bars, brothels, hospitals... you can pretty much find it being used all over the place. How many of you have heard the term VRMMO?"

Pretty much everyone raised their hands. Even I raised my hand.

"I think all of us know what a VRMMO is," Elric laughed.

"You never know," Brad said with a chuckle. "Some people have never heard the term before. I figured I'd make sure we were all on the same page before I go further." He paused to scratch his chin. "Well, anyway, what we're about to do is something very similar to a VRMMO. All of us are going to put on these suits, use a backlink to log into a place called the Rift Plains, and travel through a portal that will take us to a world currently being controlled by enemy forces."

"Hold on," Vyra said, suddenly scowling. "You mean to tell me we're... playing a video game? That's the big gig?"

I shared her sentiment, but I didn't say anything.

Brad looked at the woman with a smile, shook his head, and explained further. "What we're doing is only similar to a game, but at the same time, it's very different. The place we're traveling to is very much real. In fact, it's so real that if you die while playing this 'game,' you will die in our world. You people need to understand this fact going in. It could save your life."

I could see the skepticism written on everyone's face, and I was sure my own face looked just like theirs. Brad also seemed to realize this because he shrugged. It was like he was saying we'd find out sooner or later.

"We're using some pretty high-tech gear here," he continued. "This gear I got is all stuff that can't be found without connections. It will allow you to create an avatar that you can use for this mission. Your avatar is automatically at level 50, so you'll be able to gain some damn powerful abilities, which you're going to need thanks to where we're going. Anything less than someone at level 50 at least would be nothing but a liability. To be honest, I'm even a little worried that level 50 won't be enough, but there was nothing on the market that could give us a higher level avatar. Now, does anyone have any questions?"

"I've got one," Vyra said suddenly. "You mentioned this was a paying job, but you haven't said how much you're paying. So, how much?"

"Each of you will earn no less than 50,000, but you might make more if you do a great job. I'll be handing out bonuses to people based on their performance."

Vyra didn't say anything else as she stepped back. I could tell from the look on her face that she was satisfied. I was honestly shocked myself. We'd make 50,000 just to play a video game with this guy? No one I knew would throw that kind of money around for something so banal.

Brad must have been loaded.

"Anyone else have a question?" asked Brad. No one said anything. "Does anyone want out? If you do, now is the only chance you'll get." Again, no one said anything and no one left. Brad nodded. "In that case, let's suit up. You can put these over your clothes, but I personally recommend wearing nothing when you change."

Ju Chen and Vyra grabbed their suits and wandered off for some privacy. I didn't bother. Stripping down to my underwear, I grabbed the suit and stepped into it, pulling it over my body.

This suit appeared to be made from some kind of rubber-like fabric, but I could tell from the sensation that it wasn't rubber. It was incredibly stretchy and durable like it. However, the texture made it feel like synthetic clothes, such as polyester. After zipping the suit up, I put on gloves, boots, and grabbed the helmet, though I didn't put it on yet.

"You ready for this?" asked Elric.

I glanced at the man who was also suited up, then shrugged. "I guess."

I'd never played a VRMMO, which stood for Virtual Reality Massive Multiplayer Online. It was basically a video game you played online with hundreds of thousands or even millions of people using virtual reality technology. While I had used VR technology before to try and escape from my past, video games were not something I was into. However, that wasn't to say I'd never heard of or played them before. In my youth, I'd been damn good at Call of Duty: Space Warfare.

The women came back and Brad had all of us sit down on the recliners. Almost as soon as I sat down, the recliner lit up, the holographic screen flickering to life. It must have been using some incredible technology because it displayed my name despite how I never imputed my data. It also showed all my vital functions, pulse, blood type, heart rate, biometric rhythms, etc. I was pretty impressed, but I was also unnerved. I'm pretty sure technology like this wasn't something you could buy unless you had deep pockets.

"If everyone is ready, you should log in now," Brad called out as he placed the helmet over his head and flipped a switch near the back. His body went slack almost the moment he did so. I actually had to blink when I saw how it looked like he'd passed out or maybe even died, but I knew it was because his mind had been transported into whatever virtual world this equipment sent us to.

I stared at him, then looked at Elric, Vyra, and Ju Chen as they also placed their helmets on and flipped the switch. Like Brad, they all relaxed as if they were unconscious. Sighing as I realized I was the only one left who hadn't done so, I placed the helmet on my head, ignored the blackness filling my vision, and flipped the switch.

***

I stood in a white space. There was nothing around me at all. I couldn't tell what was up, down, left, or right. It felt almost like I was floating through an empty void. Even when I looked down, all I saw was white space. There was not even a shadow to mark where I stood.

Freaky.

As I was looking around, a screen suddenly appeared before me.

Select your race:
1. Angel
2. Demon
3. Human
4. God
5. Dragonfolk
6. Elf
7. Elder
8. Ork

Selecting an avatar, huh? This really was like one of those MMO games. After a moment of thinking, I decided to select human. Having never played an MMO before, I decided to go with what I was most familiar with. Besides, what if I selected Demon and ended up transforming into some ugly red guy with horns on my head and bat wings sticking out of my shoulders blades? I know some people thought that was cool, but I was not one of those people.

The screen changed.

You have selected the race "human." Now select your class:
1. Warrior
2. Rogue
3. Fighter
4. Monk
5. Barbarian
6. Paladin
7. Bard
8. Druid
9. Space Marine
10. Space Cadet
11. Sniper

12. Medic
13. Space Marine Commander

I stared at the list of class types, which looked like they went on forever. The list was so long I found myself scrolling down for several minutes and still hadn't reached the end. Not only did I see classic DnD classes such as Warrior, Rogue, and Paladin, but I saw sci-fi classes like Space Marine, Sniper, and Medic. It looked like someone had combined every class from every video game under the sun into a single list.

After a moment, I selected the class titled "Magic Swordsman." I honestly thought about going with one of the sci-fi classes like Space Marine, but Magic Swordsman made a bit more sense to me, since even though I wasn't huge on video games, I at least understood what a Magic Swordsman was.

The screen flickered and changed again.

Select magic color:
Red
Pink
Orange
Yellow
Green
Blue
Purple
White
Black
Brown

I frowned as I studied the colors available, but I didn't know which one I should choose. It said magic color, so I assumed different colors would mean I could use different types of magic, but I couldn't figure out which color represented what magic. Worse still, there didn't seem to be a help button or even a manual to help me out. That meant I had to choose based purely on my own guesstimation.

Not cool.

Since I could only select one color at the moment, I went with red. I was pretty sure red generally represented fire. Fire was, to me, a strong magic, and I imagined myself releasing blazing hell-like flames upon my enemies, or enhancing my sword's power with flames, allowing me to cut through enemies with a lot more ease.

The screen changed again.

Name: Bryan Jenson
Class: Magic Swordsman
Level: 50
Magic Color: Red
Attack: 0
Agility: 0
Defense: 0
Magic Defense: 0
Mana: 0
Total Status Points available: 500
Special Skills: None
Total Skill Points available: 50

I scratched my chin as I looked at the Status Points I had available. 500. Because I'd never played any RPG or MMO games, I wasn't sure if that was a big number. I was the guy who played FPS and RTS games in my youth. At the same time, I at least understood enough to know that I needed to carefully think about how I allotted my available Status Points.

After a moment, I raised Attack to 100, Agility to 100, Defense to 100, Magic Defense to 100, and Mana to 100, putting me even across the board. I figured I'd start with even stats and adjust them accordingly.

Next, I looked at my Skill Points. I had fifty available, which wasn't as big as my Status Points, but I assumed you earned one Skill Point for each level gained. After a moment of searching, I realized I couldn't see what skills I had available, but then I noticed an icon in the bottom left hand corner, which said Special Skills and had the symbol of a man holding a sword.

I selected it.

"Whoa!"

I nearly leapt back when the screen expanded to about three times its previous size. It was huge. I didn't understand why at first, but then I realized this screen revealed the Special Skills to me as a type of skill tree. There were a total of four skills currently available to me. I could tell they were the only skills I could use because they weren't grayed out like everything else.

Available Special Skills:
Whirlwind Slash: an area attack with a wide range that damages multiple opponents at the same time. Good for attacking many targets. 60 second recharge time.
Death by Piercing: Thrust your blade into a single enemy and cause critical damage. Excellent for attacking one strong enemy. Damage doubles if enemy is vulnerable to piercing damage. 30 second recharge time.
Fire Slash: Enhances blade with a flame that can be projected outward to create a ranged attack. Range depends on skill level. At level one, the skill has a range of 15 feet. 60 second recharge time.
Fireball: Shoot a fireball from your hand. Power varies depending on skill level. 30 second recharge time.

After looking over the current skills, I pressed Whirlwind Slash and allocated 5 of my 50 Skill Points to it. After reaching five, the Whirlwind Slash skill flashed several times before several other skills appeared around it. Each skill was connected to the Whirlwind Slash ability. It looked like most of them enhanced the Whirlwind Slash, but there was also one branch called Dual Whirlwind Slash. It was currently grayed out. When I followed the line connecting it to another branch, I noticed that it was connected to a skill called Dual Wielding, which I couldn't unlock until I reached level 60. So I could only use this skill if I had the dual-wielding skill.

I put five points on each of my current skills available, which dropped me down to 25 Skill Points. After that, I allocated the remaining skill points to the damage each attack inflicted per strike. My thoughts were that if I could do more damage per strike, I could kill my enemies more quickly.

After allocating all my current Skill Points to my skills, I went back to the main status screen.

Name: Bryan Jenson
Class: Magic Swordsman
Level: 50
Magic Color: Red
Attack: 100
Agility: 100
Defense: 100
Magic Defense: 100
Mana: 100
Total Status Points available: 0

Special Skills:
Whirlwind Slash: Attack +5
Death by Piercing: Attack +5
Fire Slash: Attack +5
Fireball: Attack +5
Total Skill Points available: 0

I looked everything over and nodded, satisfied with my choices. Now I just needed to know what I should do next. However, even as I wondered what I should be doing, text suddenly appeared over my status screen.

Status Allocation Complete. Do you accept? Yes? No?

As I stared at the bright "yes" and "no" buttons, I found myself hesitating just a bit, but then I pressed the "yes" button, which flashed once before the text and status screen disappeared. As the world once more turned to white, my vision flashed in and out. I wondered what was happening. However, just as this thought crossed my mind, new text flashed across my vision.

Welcome to the Rift Plains, Bryan Jenson.

Then my vision faded to black.

CHAPTER 2

I gazed around at the grassy field, completely flabbergasted and trying to figure out what the fuck just happened. One minute I was standing in a blank space. The next I was here, in this field, which looked like an idyllic prairie from some old western movie. Off in the distance I saw trees and mountains. The others had appeared with me, looking as confused as I felt.

As a soft breeze blew through the planes, causing the grass to sway and my hair to ruffle, a thought crossed my mind that I could feel the wind caressing my skin. It felt... real. It felt way too real to be a simple game. I knelt on the ground and pressed my hand against the grass, fingers splayed, feeling the soft blades rubbing against my skin. The grass also felt real.

"What. The. Fuck?" Elric's voice knocked me out of my stupor. I looked up to see him gawking at everything as well.

So, he hadn't been to... wherever this was yet. Good to know.

"Welcome, everyone. I'm glad you could all make it," Brad said. He walked over to us from a distance away, arms spread. "This place is called the Rift Plains. If you'd like, you can think of this place as a massive hotel resort with thousands of different places to go. I've come here multiple times to do some scouting before pulling together this team. We'll have to be careful. Much of these plains have already been occupied by enemy forces, but so long as we avoid the areas where enemy forces are heavily concentrated, we should be fine."

"That sounds incredibly ominous," Elric said with an awkward chuckle.

"I've already mapped out the areas with the highest concentration of enemies," Brad reassured him. "We'll be able to avoid trouble until we reach the portal."

"Before we start, I want to know a little more about what just happened," I said. "I created my character, but I can't say I understand everything."

Brad shrugged. "Ask away. If I know the answer, I will tell you."

I nodded, my eyes narrow. "When I was going through the character creation, it asked me to choose a color... what was that all about?"

"Ah." Brad's eyes lit up. "So you were able to choose a color. Very nice! The color selection system was created based on world connections. When you connect with a world through Soul Bonding, you gain a color, which represents a specific element. None of you have done that right now. You'll learn about that later if it ever becomes relevant. Your color right now is in relation to what skills you specialize in. Think of it as... selecting which elemental attribute your character has. Something along those lines."

"And this world?" asked Vyra, gesturing to the grassy plains around them. "This... Rift Plain? What is it?"

"It's like I just told you." Brad spread his arms wide. "However, if you want a more complicated version, this place is basically the starting point in this 'game' as you called it. It is a rift that leads to the many worlds of the afterlife, which you can travel to via portals. By my estimation, there are probably hundreds or maybe even thousands of portals in the Rift Plains, though don't quote me on that. Each portal leads to a different world. I've been traveling to and from this place for a while now, and I still don't know how many other worlds are out there."

Everything that came out of this man's mouth was getting harder and harder to accept, and yet... I looked around this place and couldn't help but believe him. I was a skeptic. I only believed in what I saw. If it wasn't something I could see, smell, or feel, then it obviously couldn't exist.

This place obviously existed. I could see the grassy fields, smell the earthen scent as it filled my nose, and touch the soft loam beneath me. This place, this Rift Plains, was obviously a real place. Whether or not it was the "afterlife" as Brad had called it, I couldn't say, but I could at least verify that this place was real.

"So, what are we doing?" asked Ju Chen, slinging a rifle over her shoulder.

That was when I realized all of us had changed. The changes weren't extreme... well, they were, but they weren't as extreme as I would have imagined. Ju Chen still looked very much like Ju Chen. Elric, Vyra, and Brad all had the same faces I remembered before we entered these Rift Plains. However, that was where the similarities ended.

Ju Chen was still very short, but her body was now clad in high-tech armor that vaguely reminded me of this game I had played long ago called Warhammer. Thick pauldrons sat on her shoulders, a chestplate wrapped around her torso, and strong leg guards protected her lower half. She was carrying an impressive looking rifle. I wasn't sure what it did, but it looked badass. She also had some kind of chainsaw thing strapped across her back.

Elric was dressed like a classic Paladin. His shiny steel armor was complemented by blue clothes underneath. He was wearing a tabard that trailed down the front and back, had a single pauldron on his right shoulder, and was clutching a large mace with his left hand, which was covered in a thick steel gauntlet. A shield was in his other hand. Combine that armor with his blonde hair, and he made me think of someone from Lord of the Rings.

Standing in between Ju Chen and Elric was Vyra, whose dark-skinned body was covered in... scales? Yes, they were definitely scales. Not only was she covered in scales that resembled armor, but there was a tail jutting from her lower back and large wings extending from her shoulders. The pinions held a distinctly reptilian aesthetic, making me realize she was the one person who had chosen something inhuman. I remembered reading one of the race names called Dragonfolk. I was sure that's what Vyra had chosen to be.

Brad's character was... I didn't know what he was. Clad in dark armor and chainmail blacker than midnight, his entire body seemed to exude an aura of death. While his face looked the same, everything else about him was different. What's more, he was wielding a massive scythe with jagged edges and a wicked-looking claw at the end. He was carrying a helmet under his left arm. The iron wrought helm looked like something straight out of Mordor.

I was wearing something vastly different from the norm as well. My body was covered in a type of light armor. The gleaming chestplate covered only my chest and left my stomach bare. Gauntlets and greaves covered my feet and arms, gleaming brightly in the sunlight. Black pants and a long-sleeved shirt covered me underneath my armor, and a dark cloak with blue trim had been thrown over the entire ensemble.

On top of my wardrobe change, I also had a broadsword sheathed at my waist.

"I believe I told you," Brad said with a slight smile. "Our task is going to be traveling into a world occupied by the enemy and pushing them out. A group of powerful demons have invaded a world that can be accessed from the Rift Plains. If they get any closer, it'll spell a lot of trouble for our side."

"I'm still having trouble believing any of this is real," Vyra said, her brow creased. "This is some freaky shit, and I have seen a lot of freaky shit before."

"I can assure you, it's all real," Brad said. He stabbed his scythe into the ground and scratched his head. "Now, then, before we actually do this, you guys should familiarize yourself with your equipment. You can pull up a menu screen and look over what sort of equipment you've got that way."

While everyone else was still very skeptical, all of us swiped our fingers through the air. I felt foolish as I did so, but then, to my surprise, a screen really did appear in front of me. It was small, about eight inches wide and five tall, and shaped like a rectangle. It displayed my name, an image of myself, my basic stats, and several options, including an option that said "equipment."

I pressed that option. The screen didn't change entirely. The image of me stayed there, but the stats were replaced with a list of the equipment I currently had equipped.

Equipment:
Asura Sword
Mythril chestplate
Mythril gauntlets
Mythril greaves
Nightingale Cloak
Commoners garb

While the commoners garb confused me—I assumed it was my underclothes, but the name was so drab—the rest was simple enough to understand. I'm pretty sure this was some good equipment. At least, I think it was good equipment. Mythril was always said to be a strong alloy in books and movies. According to Bilbo Baggins, mythril was harder than dragon scales.

"Have all of you familiarized yourself with your equipment?" asked Brad. "If you have, then let's go."

While Vyra grumbled a little about how none of this still made sense to her, Ju Chen just slung that badass rifle over her shoulder and marched after Brad. She seemed to be the least surprised by all this. I assume she had experience with VR games. To her, I guess, this world was just an incredibly realistic simulation.

Or maybe she was just really quick to accept things at face value.

"Pretty exciting, huh?" Elric asked as he came up to walk beside me as he, Vyra, and I began moving.

"I guess," I said with a shrug.

We made our way out of the prairie and through a forest, and it really did seem like a forest and not just an incredibly accurate simulation. The sound of chirping reached my ears. I touched the bark and felt how rough the texture was, just like a real oak tree. As we walked, our boots crunched against twigs that snapped and broke, and I could even feel minute shifts in the terrain as I stepped on roots and small bumps in the ground.

Brad seemed to be taking us on a very roundabout route. We swerved several times, cutting through clearings and passing over streams. I wasn't sure where we were going, but I remembered him mentioning enemies and how he had mapped out a route that would allow us to avoid them.

Our group eventually stopped when we reached some kind of swirling vortex. A dark eddy drifted in the air with lighter blue arcs of energy like lightning bolts drifting almost lazily out of it. It reminded me of those sci-fi shows I used to watch as a kid. As we neared this strange vortex, the hairs on the back of my neck stood on end. A shiver ran down my spine.

"Here we are," Brad said in a voice that was way too cheerful for my liking. "This is the portal. It'll take us to the world where our enemies are located. This particular portal leads to a secret passage in the other world. I found it when I was escaping after the world I was in got invaded by demons. They've only been there for a few days, so they haven't had time to solidify their power base. Our mission is to defeat all the enemies on the other side of this world, fortify the world so no one else can take it, and make this world ours."

I still had no idea what any of this meant, but I understood that we were here to fight some kind of enemy. That was enough for me. Really, fighting and killing was all I could do anyway. It was fighting, killing, and not getting killed that earned me the nickname Invincible among the Marines. Of course, sometimes I wish I had died, but that was neither here nor there.

Elric and Vyra looked about how I felt, a little uncertain now that we were finally here. I think Elric was more excited than Vyra though. Unlike Vyra, who didn't strike me as the gamer type, I knew my acquaintance was a big fan of VR games. He tried several times to convince me to play this game called *Gods End*, but I could never be bothered at the time. Now here I was, geared up in some of kind super realistic virtual reality world alongside him and several others, dressed like a freaking magical swordsman, and prepared to go on what sounded like a raid on the enemy's fortress.

It was funny how life worked out sometimes.

***

Stepping through a portal felt odd, and I mean really fucking odd. I couldn't really describe it, but it was kinda like when you wear socks and rub them against the carpet to generate static… only this was generating static all over my body. The hairs on my arms and legs bristled. My body felt like a livewire. It only lasted for a moment. Then I was out.

And my body suddenly felt incredibly cold, like someone had poured a cryogenic liquefied gas into my bloodstream.

The world around me looked nothing like the grassy plains and verdant forest I'd been standing in previously. This new place was dead. I couldn't see a single sign of plant or animal life anywhere. It looked like I was in the middle of a canyon, with massive cliffs looming over me on either side. I took a step forward. *Crunch!* Something snapped underneath my feet, and I looked down to notice I'd stepped on a skull.

A human skull.

I tried not to shudder as I walked over to Brad, carefully picking my way through several bones. He was standing a little ways in front of me. His cloak flapped in the breeze as he looked into the distance.

"The demons who've taken control over this place are quite something," Brad said as if to himself. "I've been studying these Rift Worlds for a while. This was one of the worlds I was studying when the demons attacked and forced us out. Its color is Black, in case you're curious. Black is the magic that involves spells regarding death, absorbing negativity, and darkness. This is considered a dark world. One of the people I was with had been able to Soul Bind with this world and could use those powers as he pleased. He's dead now, though. The demons killed him when they attacked."

As he spoke, the others arrived, first Elric, then Ju Chen, and finally Vyra. All of them shivered like I had when I first arrived here. However, I only paid them a cursory glance. Most of my attention was focused on Brad.

"Soul Binding is that thing you talked about before," I said.

Brad nodded. "You can basically bind yourself to different worlds. If you bind yourself to a world, you'll gain that world's color, and your ability to use magic represented by that color will increase. The darker your color is, the stronger your magic becomes. You can also summon beings from a world you are Soul Bound to." He paused. "But you can't do that right now, since that's not the real you. It's just an avatar."

"Interesting," I said, mostly because I didn't have anything else to say. "Wait. What do you mean the real me?"

But Brad didn't answer me.

"It looks like everyone is here," Brad murmured as he turned to look back at all of us. "All right. Since we're all here, let's keep going. This portal dropped us off close to a secret entrance I plan on using to have us enter the fortress. I actually used that portal to escape last time. Had I not... well, let's just say I probably wouldn't be here right now."

With Brad in the lead, we continued marching on. The barren ground, high cliffs, and lack of life was was so vastly different from what I had experienced before that it was hard to wrap my head around everything. That was why I shunted all these thoughts aside and tried to focus on the mission.

We eventually reached what appeared to be a giant wall built into the cliff. Brad walked up to it, tapped on the wall several times, and then reached a point where the wall sounded hollow. He grinned and pushed on the wall. It moved inward, a loud grinding sound echoing from it, as it revealed a dark passageway.

"Ju, that rifle of yours has a flashlight, right?" asked Brad.

"It does." Ju Chen walked to the front, turned on her flashlight, and performed a very professional sweep of the inside. What little I could see beyond her revealed a stone floor and walls. It looked like a dark hallway to some fantasy-esque dungeon.

"You lead us from here," Brad said to her. "I'd do it myself, but I don't have a light."

Ju Chen didn't complain. Nodding once, she walked into the passage and the rest of us followed. I glanced around at the walls and ceiling, but aside from looking like an ancient building made of large stone, it didn't seem all that special. Even so, walking through such a dark passage caused the hairs on my arm to prickle.

The passageway soon ended in a door. Brad took the lead after that, opening the door and walking through. We followed him and discovered a staircase on the other side. It wasn't very big. I'd say two of us would be able to walk up it standing shoulder to shoulder —except for maybe Vyra, whose broad shoulders were about two people altogether.

Our footsteps echoed ominously through the staircase as we ascended higher and higher, until we eventually reached the end, where a wall stood before us. It was a dead end. However, even as I thought that, Brad once more pushed the wall aside and walked through.

What lay on the other side was a long hallway. The stone floor, walls, and ceiling made this place look like an ancient fortress I once saw when I was traveling through Europe. Candles lit the way, situated on the wall at even intervals. There were no windows, no decorations, just a long hallway.

"It looks like this is our lucky day," Brad said with a grin. "There are no patrols in this area yet, though we need to be quick."

"Hey, if our job is to take this base from the enemy, why are we sneaking around?" asked Vyra, scowling.

"Because in order to make this base ours, what we need to do isn't just clear out the enemy. We need to find the Dungeon Master as well. We find the Dungeon Master, take them out, and then clear out the rest. It will be easier with the DM gone. He'll be the most powerful fucker in this whole place, so if we can defeat him, the rest of the baddies will be mostly grunts. The only person we'll need to fight before the DM is a succubus who's kind of like the mini-boss of this particular area. She's a right bitch and quite vicious. I want to avoid making too much noise and alerting her to our presence. It will make things harder if she knows we are here."

"Well, I suppose that's fair enough," Vyra admitted.

"Right. So, let's go."

And so off we went, traveling down the long corridor, which branched off into multiple other corridors. We didn't run into any of those demons Brad had mentioned.

At least, not at first.

It happened while we were turning a corner. A pair of small creatures, clearly not human, also turned the corner at merely the same time. They only came up to about my waist, had crimson skin covered in cracks, and glowing eyes the color of blood. Horns curved around their heads. Their hands only had three fingers with wicked claws, wings jutted from their backs, and they had a spaded tail swinging behind them.

"Oh, shit. Imps. Bryan! You and me! Let's take 'em!" Brad shouted as he rushed forward and swung his scythe. His weapon cleaved clean through the imp nearest him. The creature was sliced in half before it exploded into dust—perhaps ash.

I'd never used a sword before, but I pulled it from my sheathe, ran forward, and thrust it out like I would an army knife. The blade pierced an imp's head. I felt my blade slide through with a bit of resistance, saw blood gush from the head wound, and then the imp burst into ash like the first one.

I thought that was the end of it, but then loud squawking came from behind us. It was another one of those imps. No, there wasn't just one. Several sets of glowing red eyes appeared in the distance. Dozens even. They stood shoulder to shoulder, wings retracted, eyes glaring at us with a malevolence that caused me to feel like knives were penetrating my flesh. One of them squawked, then the rest squawked, and then they all began rushing toward us.

"Shit! This isn't good," Brad snapped. "Everybody, prepare for enemy contact! If any of you have any buffing spells, now's the time to use them."

All of us readied ourselves for battle. I gripped my sword, Elric his mace and shield, Ju Chen her gun, and Vyra's claws suddenly seemed to elongated and sharpen. Elric then lifted his mace, which began glowing with a bright white light. I wasn't sure what happened, exactly, but as he did this, my body suddenly felt... lighter. It was as if I weighed a little less than before... no, more like I felt stronger than before.

This must be a buff.

Seconds before the horde of imps made contact, Ju Chen dropped to her knees, took aim, and opened fire. Her gun spat bullets at a rapid rate, mowing down the first line of imps. They collapsed to the ground and didn't get up. Then they burst into dust just like the other imps had. The rest of the imps continued rushing toward our group like hungry wolves attacking a pack of helpless sheep. Ju Chen kept firing, but it was clear she'd never be able to kill them all.

And then the imps reached us.

I swung my sword like I'd seen people do in movies. It felt awkward and clumsy. Marines weren't trained to use a sword, though we were trained to use just about every other weapon under the sun, including utensils. Even though I wasn't what I would have called graceful, swinging a sharp object wasn't very hard. My sword cleaved through imps with ease as I swung it around.

As I began fighting, I remembered those skills I had: Whirlwind Slash, Death by Piercing, Fire Slash, and Fireball. As I shuffled backward to avoid a claw, which came inches to hitting me in the face, I thought about the Fireball skill and how nice it would be if I could just burn all these creatures to cinders.

Almost like the magic responded to my will, I felt a pull on my lower stomach. It felt like something was being drained from me. Then a spark exploded above my head, transforming into a small conflagration that shot forward, striking a group of imps further back and incinerating them. The explosions wasn't very big. It didn't even damage the ground. However, six imps were blasted apart, bursting into ash as they died.

Wow. That was pretty cool.

I wasn't the only one using magic. Elric slammed his mace into the ground, creating a quake effect that knocked the imps near him away. It didn't spread far. However, even my body rumbled as the attack struck me. I couldn't feel myself take any damage or suffer an injury, so I assumed it hadn't reached me, but it looked like friendly fire was possible here.

"There are too many of them!" Ju Chen shouted.

"Let's retreat!" Brad called out.

The five of us began a fighting retreat with me and Vyra in the rear. The woman who had turned herself into a Dragonfolk was even more vicious than her species was known for in most media. She killed creatures with claw and tail. Some of the imps unfortunate enough to come near her were slammed into the wall with her tail, their bones shattering. Ash burst all around her as she demolished the imps that attacked her.

I used my sword to carve up several imps that got too close. I wanted to try that attack of mine, Whirlwind Slash, which was said to be good against multiple enemies at once, but I didn't have the time to use it. Despite this, imps burst into ash as I killed them, and I felt something odd rush into me each time. I didn't know what it was. I didn't have time to figure it out either.

We reached the end of this corridor, which led to a set of double doors. Brad was the first inside. The rest of us followed him. We slammed the door shut.

"Get something to bar the entrance!" Vyra shouted.

I looked around the cylindrical room we found ourselves in, but I couldn't see anything we could use to block the entrance. There was a large statue in the center of the room. It was of a man having his heart pulled out of his chest by a naked woman with devil wings and a spaded tail. There were also a number of tall columns that reached up to the ceiling several dozen feet above us. Candles sat in small candle holders to illuminate the room. That was about it.

"There's nothing here," Elric came to the same conclusion.

"Fuck!" shouted Vyra.

All of us leapt away from the door as something slammed into it. The door exploded, and the imps poured in, leaving us with no choice but the keep fighting.

CHAPTER 3

I was caught in the middle of a blood bath. Imps stormed into this cylindrical room, shrieking with laughter as they attacked us, and we cut them down with superior strengths and skills. Blood ran along my blade, arced through the air, and drenched the ground, creating slippery puddles that we had to be mindful of if we didn't want to fall. Falling now could prove fatal. The imps would overwhelm us with sheer numbers.

Taking a stance with my feet spread, sword extended, I channeled mana through my blade and called upon the skill I wanted to use. A slight tug at my gut was the prelude to my attack. I spun around, a full 360 degrees, and a powerful arc of red energy shot out in a full circle like a single ripple spreading across a lake.

The first group of imps surrounding me were mowed down. Blood sprayed from their bodies as they fell. The imps fell to the ground as they were cut in half, then their bodies burst into ash and a strange form of energy filled me. My energy attack continued on, cutting through two more groups of imps, though my attack lost power the further it went from me. While the second group died same as the first, the last group only received light cuts.

Several yards from me, Vyra was tearing into the imps surrounding her with claws, feet, and tail. It was impressive. Using nothing more than brute strength, she launched imps through the air. They soared across the sky and smacked into their fellow imps, taking them all down in a jumble of limbs. Most of her attacks sounded like explosions. Each strike echoed through the room, each hit seemed to break the imp she struck.

Elric and Brad were fighting side by side. Scythe and mace swept imps away in twos and threes. As a Paladin, Elric had a lot of physical strength on top of his holy abilities. His mace glowed as he swung, crushing skulls, knocking imps away, and breaking their bodies. Meanwhile, Brad swung his scythe in wide arcs, slicing off limbs, cutting imps in half, and slowly whittling down their numbers.

Behind them was Ju Chen, the Space Marine who was using the pair as cover, while she took potshots at any target of opportunity. Her aim was impeccable. Every shot was a headshot. I was fighting one of the imps, and one had come up behind me, when Ju Chen put a bullet through the creature's head. It flew back and hit the ground, rolling to a stop and tripping several of its comrades before exploding into ash.

I had no idea how long we'd been fighting. The stench of blood made my nose curl. We kept fighting and killing, but no matter how many imps we slaughtered, more kept coming.

This was too real, I concluded. I'd been sure this was all some kind of realistic virtual reality simulation, but there was no way an experience like this could be simulated to such an astounding degree of accuracy. This was real. The weight of the sword, the feeling of resistance when I cleaved through an imp. Whatever this world was, whatever these creatures were, they were no illusion, no mere simulation.

I was forced to accept what Brad had been telling us.

As the situation continued, as our battle progressed, a loud rumbling echoed from some distance away, growing louder with each passing second. Once the room began to shake, the imps all screeched in fear and ran off. It was so sudden and startling that none of us could figure out what was happening.

"What the hell?" Elric asked, scratching his head.

"Something is coming," Vyra said, almost hissing as she glanced around in fear.

"Whatever is coming, it's a lot bigger and more powerful than those imps," Ju Chen added as she looked toward the door.

Brad said nothing, but his eyes had turned toward the door, and I looked over just in time to see something large and hulking standing behind it—before the entire door was blown inward.

What blasted through the door stood on two legs. It had a large frame covered in thick, corded muscles. Scars crossed its body. It wasn't wearing much in the way of clothes. A loincloth wrapped around its torso to protect its modesty. Motley green skin reminiscent of leather gleamed in the dull light. This creature was bald and had no eyebrows, but prominent brow-ridges combined with sharp tusk-like teeth jutting from its lower lip gave it a mean look. As it spotted us, the creature opened its mouth, raised a wicked-looking ax over its head, and roared as it charged forward.

"OGRE!" Ju Chen shouted in shock.

As the creature charged, Vyra and I darted away from each other. The ogre raced past us, the rumbling of its steps causing my body to shake. It charged at Elric and Brad. The paladin and the death knight leapt away as well. Ju Chen also tried to scramble out of the way, but she was a tad too slow.

I watched in horror as the ogre swung his ax in a wide, horizontal arc, his weapon catching Ju Chen in the torso. Her mouth was open in a scream as her body was split in half. Her torso went flying, spinning through the air, before it landed on the ground with a wet, meaty thud. She still seemed to be alive, barely, but then the ogre grabbed her torso, raised her to his mouth, and bit down.

My insides churned and tried to regurgitate my dinner as a sickening crunch echoed around us. Blood spilled over the ogre's mouth as it ate Ju Chen, tearing off pieces of her flesh and crunching down on the bones. All of us were too shocked by what happened to do anything more than watch. Even when I was in the Marines, I had never seen anything this violent or disgusting.

The moment soon passed. The ogre, finished with its meal, turned to us.

"If you have a buff, use it now! Close range fighters attack, but be careful of its ax and don't let it grab you!" Brad shouted. "Use special attacks skills if you have them!"

At those words, I snapped back to myself and tightened my grip on the sword in my hand. Now wasn't the time to be shocked or get queasy.

I was the first to overcome my disgust. Racing forward, I released a furious roar as I pictured the skill I wanted to use. The strange draining sensation when I used mana engulfed me as my blade was coated in a bright red energy, and then I was thrusting my sword forward. Death by Piercing. My blade sank into the stomach of the ogre, though it couldn't go up to the hilt. The further in my sword got, the harder it became to move. Blood dripped from around the blade as it stopped moving. I grimaced and tried to pull it out, only it wouldn't come out.

"Look out, Bryan!"

A shout was my only warning, but it was all I needed to let go of my sword and drop to the ground.

A moment later, something passed over my head, so fast I could barely see it. As I stood back up, the ogre's arm had stopped. I noticed the ax in its hand, an ax which was coming back down for a return swing.

I leapt backward as fast as I could. The ax missed, but I could feel it passing through where I had been. A gust of wind pushed against me, showing me how powerful this attack was. If that thing hit me, I would die.

As I leapt back, Vyra and Elric came in from the left and right. They attacked in unison. Elric's glowing white mace slammed into the ogre, and Vyra's claws, which looked like they had caught fire, slashed into its left flank. The ogre roared in agony as it spun around and tried to take them out. Vyra and Elric proved faster than it was, however, and moved back.

In that moment, Brad came in with a powerful swing of his scythe, which was coated in a viscous black flame. Something about that flame gave me chills. I couldn't understand it, but there was a sense of wrongness, of death, that I felt emanating from it. Whatever that flame was, it allowed Brad's scythe to easily slice through the creature. Blood gushed from the new wound he opened, splashing onto the floor.

The ogre must have been on its deathbed. It lurched forward and cupped its stomach as though trying to keep its organs from spilling out, but then its arms sagged and it pitched forward, hitting the ground with a loud rumble that shook the room. Its body twitched a few times, but then it went completely still.

"Is everyone okay?" asked Brad.

"I'm okay," Elric said.

"I'm glad one of us is," Vyra snapped. "I'm not okay. And what about Ju Chen? Is she going to be okay? Will she respawn or —"

"I wish that were the case," Brad said as I walked up to the troll and grabbed my sword, still embedded into the creature's strong hide. "However, I told you this already. Dying in this world means dying in our world."

"Fuck this shit!" Vyra screamed. "I'm out! I'm done with this!" She pulled up her screen and began pressing something. I couldn't see what it was, but after a moment, the blood drained from her somewhat reptilian face as she looked from the screen to Brad. "I can't log out! Why can't I log out?"

"I told you that your last chance to turn back was in the Rift Plains," Brad informed her. "You cannot log out when you're in a world that has been occupied by enemy forces. If you want to log out, the only way to do so is to defeat the Dungeon Master and clear the world of enemies."

Vyra's face paled further. Meanwhile, Elric looked like he had suddenly swallowed something extremely foul. I felt about the same as they looked.

"How does that even work?!" asked Vyra with a cry of frustration.

I pulled my blade free of the ogre's hide and turned to Brad, eager to hear what he had to say about this matter. To his credit, Brad looked calm as he ran a hand through his hair.

"I don't know the full details myself, but a company tried to create a simulation that would allow users to interact with their lost loved ones. It was supposed to be something people used to get closure." He sighed, shook his head, and continued. "But something went wrong. They went too far, and suddenly, portals began opening all over the world. These portals connect to the afterlife... an afterlife... or maybe even every afterlife. I'm not sure on those details. All I know for sure is that the Rift Plains we started off in is connected to dozens, hundreds, or maybe even thousands of worlds, many of which have hostile enemies like the creatures we're fighting here."

"Why has no one heard of this?" asked Elric. "If something like this happened, then surely someone would have said something, right?"

As the conversation continued, the ogre we had fought broke down and turned to dust, but it left several items that I strode toward and picked up. One of them was a large tusk. The other object was its ax. As I picked both objects up, they disappeared in a flash, and a soft dinging sound alerted me that something had happened seconds before a screen appeared in front of me.

Item Drops:
Ax of Uruk
Ogre Tusk

"There are obviously people who have heard about it," Brad said, gesturing toward himself. "However, the government has done a good job of keeping everything covered for the moment. Imagine the panic, the chaos that would spread if people learned a rift had opened between our world and other words." Brad looked at where Ju Chen's lower half was lying and grimaced. "In either case, that's why I hired you guys for this job. The place we're in now is one of those worlds, a lesser world that was recently overrun by powerful demons. This world is close to the Rift Plains."

"I understand." I turned to look at Brad, my eyes narrowed. "Basically, if something isn't done to clear these demons out of this world, they could overrun the Rift Plains and eventually make it to our world. That about sums it up, right?"

"Yes." Brad nodded.

"So what do we do now?" asked Vyra.

"We keep moving," Brad said, shrugging.

None of us could say anything against his idea.

***

We moved on, fighting enemies as we went. Most of what we ran into were low-level imps. They appeared to be the grunts in this base, easy to kill but attacked in hordes. Sometimes we ran into stronger monsters, but the strongest creature we'd had to fight so far aside from ogres were succubus.

Succubus were a type of female demon who appeared as gorgeous women with large breasts, wide hips, and a perfect waist. Their clothing always left little to the imagination. Most of the succubus we ran into had armor that looked like they were made with seduction in mind instead of protection. They had different color skin, sometimes red, sometimes pink, and sometimes purple or blue. The color of their skin seemed to denote what kind of attacks they used.

"It's a pink one!" Brad shouted. "Vyra, you're up!"

A gorgeous monster with soft pink skin walked over to us from down the hall with a sensual sway of her hips. She was nearly naked. Her breasts bounced as she walked. The tail sprouting from just above her perfect ass swayed from side to side like an inverted pendulum. Her tail ended in a trident shape that made it look like a weapon. Pouty lips. A small nose. Seductively narrowed crimson eyes. Even from a distance, I could feel something tugging at my libido.

We men stepped back as Vyra raced forward. Her feet pounded against the stone floor, leaving dents in their wake as she barreled toward the female demon. The woman unleashed a ferocious roar as she threw a punch at the succubus. Her attack missed when the demon leapt backward. She was surprisingly nimble. After avoiding the powerful attack, the creature blew Vyra a kiss.

While it seemed like she was taunting Vyra at first, I knew that was not the case. A small pink heart flew toward Vyra, who dodged left and allowed it to pass her, then came forward and threw a fist. Her attack hit this time. I could actually hear the smacking of her fist against the succubus's face. The attack was so powerful it blasted the succubus off her feet and sent her crashing into a wall, which cracked upon impact.

It didn't get back up.

The succubus soon burst into ashes.

"I'm glad we came up with a strategy to deal with those things," Elric said as they turned a corner. "I really don't want to be on the receiving end of those charm powers again."

"That was pretty embarrassing, wasn't it?" I asked with a slight chuckle. "I've never seen a person drool over someone in real life like that."

Elric shuddered. "Please don't remind me."

Our footsteps echoed down the hall, which ended in a large door. Something about this door seemed... ominous. Perhaps it was the size. Up to this point, most of the doors we had wandered through were small single doors. This one was a double door that spanned the entire width of the hallway, towered over us by a good several feet, and looked like it was made from human bones. I saw skulls and rib cages embedded in the door, surrounded by femurs and other bones, all combined into a horrifying meshwork that made me think this was a gateway that led straight to Hell.

"It looks like we've reached the first checkpoint," Brad murmured. "Beyond this point is what I've taken to calling a sub-boss. Think of sub-bosses as a secondary boss that is less powerful than the main boss but still stronger than the average grunt on this level. If we can defeat this boss, we'll be able to continue on to the next area. Fortunately, all of us are level 50, which is a pretty damn high level."

"What level are the creatures on this floor?" I asked.

Brad cocked his head to the side. "About level 30 or 40, I'd say. I'm not sure since I don't have the scan ability. The only reason Ju Chen lost her life to that ogre is because it caught us by surprise. Damage is dealt differently in this world than it is in a video game.

No matter how high the level, if you get cut with an ax being swung from an ogre, unless your body is made of metal or something, you're gonna die."

All of us nodded.

With his explanation finished, Brad walked up to the door and pushed it open, the door groaning like humans screaming in pain. What lay on the other side of this door was a massive room with columns lining the walls. A stairway stood on the other side. However, in front of the stairway was a throne, and sitting on that throne was a woman.

It was another succubus.

Dark blue skin covered every inch of her luscious frame. She sat with one leg crossed over the other, supple muscles flexing as she changed from leaning her head on her left hand to leaning it on her right hand. Strange yellow lines like symbols or runes covered her skin, glowing brightly in the room. She stood up, her impressively large breasts jiggling within the confines of her metal top, which looked like clawed hands grasping her tits. That had to be uncomfortable, but the woman paid no attention as if she didn't notice. She was barefoot, a spaded tail jutted from her lower back, wings extended and retracted, and the horns on her head resembled a heart-shaped crown.

She was the first succubus we had run into that possessed wings. I wondered if there was some significance in that.

"I was wondering what the commotion was," she said, lips curving into a smile. I blinked. This was the first time I'd heard one of these demons talk. Her voice was husky and deep, containing a smoky and seductive quality that I was sure any man would have loved to hear screaming their name in bed. "So you've returned, and you brought friends."

"You didn't think I'd stay away." Brad shrugged and smirked at the woman. "You and your people have come too close to the

Rift Plains. I can't have you invading our world, so you're gonna have to go."

The woman snorted, but her lips curled into an amused and sexy smile. "You can't delay the inevitable. No matter how many people you bring, no matter how hard you fight, nothing will change... or have you forgotten about what happened the last time you were here?"

"I haven't forgotten." Brad's eyes hardened. "I learned my lesson last time. This time I brought more capable people."

The woman—succubus—narrowed her eyes. "We shall see."

She raised a hand and snapped her fingers, and then the walls on either side opened to reveal hidden passages, from which dozens of creatures stormed out. Most of them were imps. However, next to the imps were four massive ogres and two succubi. Both of the succubi were a deep red color. Their eyes glowed with a furious power like fire was hidden behind them, just waiting to burst free. Neither of them had wings, but they both had a tail, one spaded and the other forked.

With these forces arrayed against us, our own forces stumbled back.

"This does not look good," Vyra muttered. She sounded like she was beginning to regret accepting this job. I sort of understood how she felt.

"You know how in video games, you always fight the bosses with your party and don't have to worry about random enemies attacking you from behind?" asked Elric.

"Yeah." My eyes narrowed as I judged our enemies. There were twenty in total. Minus the two succubi (three if I included the sub-boss) and four ogres, that made for a total of twelve imps. "What about it?"

"I miss those days," Elric confided.

I snorted.

Then the battle commenced.

The imps came first, releasing their wretched battle-cries as they charged at us. Brad didn't bother with them as he raced forward, his death scythe spinning about like the propellers of a helicopter. Several imps were slaughtered when they got too close. His charge took him past the imps, passed the two succubi and four ogres, and straight toward the sub-boss. The woman cackled as she suddenly disappeared from sight and some sort of large monster sprang forth as though summoned from the depths of Hell.

I had no time to watch him since the imps came at us. I felt the drain on my mana as I created a large fireball in front of me and swung my sword. My sword caught fire, then the fire blasted off my blade in a wide arc that caught five imps. The flaming crescent blade sliced through them. Combine with the imps Brad had killed, there were now only nine—make that six. Elric had just destroyed three with his mace.

The imps were easy enough to slay, but once we had killed them off, the ogres and succubi came next. Massive rumbling shook the room as the ogres stomped forward and attacked us. All four of them were wielding massive axes. They swung them hard, but we moved away to dodge them. However, we soon found ourselves with another problem.

The succubi.

Heat washed over me as a fireball slammed into my chest. I screamed as I felt the fire burning me, even through my armor. It hurt. By fucking God, it hurt unlike anything I'd felt before. I was blasted off my feet and struck the ground hard, rolling for several yards. Scrambling to my feet, I barely had time to avoid the swing of another ax as one of the ogres bore down on me.

I raced between the creature's legs. As I did, I activated Fire Slash again, felt the drain on my mana, and swung my sword. There was a moment of resistance, but then my sword cleaved through the creature's left leg in a spray of blood and flames. The monster roared as it went down. I paid it no mind, since it couldn't do anything with a missing leg, and instead looked toward my companions.

One other ogre lay dead on the ground, its head severed from its body, but the remaining two were harassing Elric and Vyra. Fortunately, Vyra had a strong fire element and seemed resistant to the succubi's flames. However, Elric was not doing so well. He had to constantly run across the ground as fireballs flew around him from all sides. He was also forced to dodge the ogres, who attacked with a relentless tenacity.

I thought about what I needed to do for a moment, and then charged toward one of the succubus.

She didn't notice my approach at first, busy as she was toying with Elric. By the time she did notice me, it was too late. Death by Piercing. I thrust my blade into her chest. Her eyes widened as blue blood spilled from the wound around my sword, which went through her chest and out her back. She looked down at the weapon like she couldn't believe what she was seeing. I didn't care. I pulled my blade free with a jerk and watched as she fell back with a thud. Her body remained there for several seconds before it burst apart. The strange sensation of being filled up with something rushed through me, then disappeared.

Now there was only one succubus and two more ogres.

I glanced at Brad, who was battling against the strange monster that succubus had summoned, and I couldn't help but grimace. Brad looked awful. His armor was missing in several places. Blood flowed freely from wounds on his arms, face, and legs. One of his arms looked like it had been rendered useless somehow. It hung limply at his side, forcing him to fight with only one hand, which hampered his fighting effectiveness.

Then I looked at Vyra and Elric. The two of them were having an easier time than before, but it was still hard going. They dodged swings from the two ogres, and the succubus had decided to focus her attacks on Elric, who wasn't immune to fire like Vyra seemed to be. One of the flames struck him, and he went down with a scream.

Making another decision, I raced toward Elric and Vyra. I ran toward the nearest ogre and leapt into the air. Maybe it was because I was at a high level, but my leap took me clear above its head, and as I came down from above, I used Death by Piercing to penetrate its skull. My sword went through the back of its head and out its mouth. I pulled the blade free, leapt down from its shoulders, and landed on the ground.

I paid no attention to the creature as it fell to the floor, but I felt how it shook the room.

Vyra was able to take care of the other ogre. She flew into the air and clawed at its throat. Blood gushed from the wound before she plunged her claws into its eye socket as it went down. Meanwhile, Elric had finally used a spell that shot a white beam of energy from his mace, which struck the succubus and caused her to scream as her body burst into black ash.

We glanced at each other, to confirm that all of us were okay, then joined Brad, who looked even more like shit than before. It seemed as if he had slain the monster, which had disappeared. However, the succubus who had re-appeared, as though she was done hiding, looked pristine.

She smiled at them.

"Oh, my. You took care of those creatures fast." The succubus held a hand to her cheek. "I wasn't expecting you to kill those grunts for at least another few minutes."

Brad wore a pained expression as he reached into his cloak and pulled out a flask of bubbling red liquid, which he downed in a single swig. My eyes widened as his wounds healed in front of me.

It was like someone had reversed the flow of time, like watching a movie in rewind. His arm knit back together, his cuts disappeared, and even the blood covering his body vanished.

"You're outnumbered now," Brad said. "There's no way you can win against all of us."

"You think so?" The succubus grinned.

Her confident expression unnerved me. She really was outnumbered now, and even if she had no trouble against one of us, there was no way she could defeat all of us. She had to know that. Even if she was bluffing, there should have been some hint that she was nervous. Yet as I looked at her face, I couldn't see a single hint of worry on her succulent features.

A loud rumbling suddenly caused the floor to shake. I thought another ogre was coming at first, but then a creature emerged from the stairway. Far larger than even the ogres had been, at least twice their size, this monstrosity was covered from head to toe in what appeared to be bone armor. It had two legs and two thick arms like tree trunks, bulging with veins. A pair of claymores was gripped within its massive hands. Gleaming red eyes glowed with malevolence from beneath an iron wrought helm that resembled a demon.

"I knew you'd be back, so I made a playmate for you," she said. "He takes a little while to activate, though, so I had to distract you with those grunts and a few parlor tricks. However, he is now ready to play with you. I hope you can all become good friends with him."

As I stared at this massive creature, so far beyond my comprehension, I wondered about how powerful it was. Surely it didn't have the same strength as this sub-boss. However, it must have been strong. It looked strong, at least.

I looked at Brad. His expression was pale. All the blood had drained from his face, but his eyes were hard as he gripped his scythe.

"Anyone have any ideas?" asked Elric. None of us said anything. "Well, shit."

And that was when the creature charged. It moved faster than I thought possible. Brad tried to stop it, but it swung one of its claymores at him. He raised his scythe to block. However, trying to block a swing like that was impossible. While Brad wasn't sliced in half, his body was picked up and hurtled through the air like a ragdoll before he smacked the floor. I thought he'd be out, but he sprang back to his feet surprisingly quickly and charged forward again.

The rest of this battle became a blur to me as we attacked this creature, were repelled, and then had to dodge its counterattacks. Those heavy swings it used dug gouges in the floor. Each attack was a one-hit kill, so we had to avoid all of them. We couldn't even afford to block, lest we get sent flying like Brad first did.

The woman watched on, arms crossed under her breasts, a pleased smile on her face. However, she seemed to become disinterested in merely standing there and soon joined the fray. Once that happened, our situation became impossible.

The woman herself was not a close-range fighter. She disappeared like a ghost and attacked with magic from a distance. I couldn't tell what she specialized in, but she hit Vyra with a strange spell that made the woman drop to her knees and scream in fear. She would have died when the bone knight swung its sword at her. However, Elric and I grabbed the Dragonfolk woman and leapt back mere seconds before the sword plowed into the ground.

"It's no good. Damn it! Retreat!" Brad soon came to realize we weren't strong enough to fight this monster and the succubus.

We started running backward, but the succubus was having none of that.

"Oh, no, no, no. You can't leave after coming all this way to visit. At least stay for tea and cookies."

As she spoke, more imps, ogres, and succubi emerged from those secret passages and tried to block our way. We cut into them, but there were so many it was like wading through cement. With the monster and sub-boss behind us and these beasts in front, we were shit out of luck.

Visions of my past played before me as the other three fought as ferociously as they could. My friends dying all around me, my hands stained red as I tried to save them. Helplessness. Coldness. Isolation. All the emotions I felt back then were coming back to me in waves, but rather than let them take me, I used them to fuel me. I knew what I had to do.

I would not let anyone die again.

With a roar, I jumped into the fray and activated Whirlwind Slash. Blood sprayed around me like a fine mist as several imps were cut down and an ogre lost its leg. Then I activated Fire Slash, decimating even more forces in front of us, followed by Fireball. My quick succession of attacks cleared a path for my comrades.

"Everybody run!" I shouted.

No one argued. They ran as I activated Death by Piercing and killed an ogre by impaling it through the throat. My cooldown time for Whirlwind Slash went down, so I used it again to kill more demons.

By this point, my comrades had already reached the door. They pushed it open and ran out. However, Elric turned to me as I activated Fire Slash again.

"Come on! Hurry!" he shouted at me.

I decimated another group with Fireball, then turned around and tried to run, but the moment I took another step forward, a wave of dizziness swept over me. I blinked, then blinked again. Before I realized what was happening, I had fallen face first onto the floor. Darkness began surrounding me. I thought I heard a scream. Then my world faded away.

Everything went black.

CHAPTER 4

It felt like someone had smacked me over the head with a hammer. As I woke up, releasing a stifled groan of pain, I wondered what the hell I'd been drinking last night to get such a bad hangover. Not only did it feel like my head had been split open and someone broke my brains apart with a jackhammer, but my arms and shoulders felt like they'd been torn from their sockets.

A cold breeze blew over my body, making me shiver, and I wondered if whoever I'd slept with last night had stolen the blanket. This was the last time I was sleeping with that—

"Oh. I think he is finally coming to," a voice said, causing my thoughts to freeze.

I opened my eyes and looked around. I couldn't see much. Everything appeared as fuzzy shapes, but as I blinked, the world eventually came into sharp focused, and I realized this was not some woman's bedroom, there was no blanket, and I was not lying in a bed. I wasn't even lying down.

I was hanging from the ceiling, my arms bound in shackles. That dull ache I felt came from my arms having to carry the entire weight of my body for who knew how long.

"Good morning," a woman said to me. She had a face that was pleasing to look at. Her soft nose was small and cute, and her full, sensuous lips were pursed as they curled into a smile that made me tempted to lean down and kiss them. Seductively narrowed eyes that glowed a soft blue stared at me from a pink face—as in a face that was literally pink and not just blushing. What's more, her eyes were not just blue. The iris, sclera, and even her pupil were all one uniform color. Also, she had horns on her head.

Which just brought another point home.

This woman wasn't human.

"What... what is...?"

I tried to ask "What the hell is going on?" but couldn't. My throat felt thick, like something was clogging it, and that made it hard to talk.

"I wouldn't try to speak just yet." The woman smiled, though it wasn't a very kind smile. It was more amused than anything. "You ended up expanding all your mana and suffered from what we call Mind Down. It happens when you use up every ounce of mana you have. Your mind shuts down temporarily until your mana recovers." She paused, her smile widening. "You know, you are quite lucky my mistress is so magnanimous. When she saw you pass out, she decided to take you captive rather than kill you. Aren't you fortunate?"

While she said that like I should consider myself lucky, the fact that she said I was being held captive caused me to remember what happened to me. I remembered accepting a job, traveling into this not-virtual reality world, fighting through a horde of monsters, and battling against this succubus creature and her minions. Nothing after that though. It was like there was a blank space in my memories, likely caused by that Mind Down thing this demon lady just mentioned.

"What... do you plan on doing with me?" I asked.

The succubus's smile widened. "Good question. You see, my mistress actually wants to know about your world, and she has given me the savory—I mean, the honorable task of prying that information from your lips."

"So you mean to interrogate me," I said.

"Correct."

There were a lot of things I could have said and done in response to that. I could have told her I'd never say anything, could have spat in her face, could have told her to suck my dick—which admittedly was a thought. I didn't, however. No, it was more like I couldn't.

The succubus woman stared at me, the glow in her eyes brightening, and she suddenly looked ten—no, a hundred times more attractive than before. I realized only now that she wasn't wearing any clothing. Her completely naked body was bared before me, inch after inch of supple flesh that I just wanted to grab. Perky tits that were large and seemed to completely defy gravity made me wish I could lean forward and take her nipples into my mouth. In this moment, the woman before me was a beauty unlike any other. It felt like I was falling in love.

"Tell me what you know about your world," the woman said. Her voice contained a seductive overtone that made me want to tell her. "What's it like? What are the people like? Is there a military infrastructure we need to be aware of?"

I opened my mouth to answer her. It was an unconscious gesture, but then I quickly snapped it shut. I closed my eyes to block out the sight of this woman. Even though I was trapped within a haze of lust, I realized, however belatedly, that she was doing something to my mind, making me so horny and enamored with her that I wanted to reveal all my secrets.

"Come on now." Something grabbed my eyelids and pried them open. I tried to close them, but I couldn't. "It's okay. You can tell me."

The woman gave me this reassuring smile, as if everything would be all right if I told her what I knew, that telling her what I knew would make everything better. It felt like an incredible pressure was welling up inside of my mind. All of my mental energy, everything I could dredge up, was being used to resist that smile.

In a last ditch effort to resist this compulsion, I gathered the saliva in my mouth and spat in the woman's face.

The compulsion disappeared. The smile on the woman's face was gone.

"Ungrateful bastard!" she screeched. "I tried to be nice! I tried to do this the easy way, the pleasant way, but it seems like more drastic measures will be needed!"

At these words, the woman raised her hand, and I noticed that she had some incredibly long nails. Sharp. Pointed. Those things were no joke. Of course, I only realized what they were going to be used for as she brought her hand down and raked those nails against my flesh.

I bit my lip to keep from screaming in pain, though I couldn't stop myself from whimpering. Blood welled up along my skin as the woman's nails tore into me. Four ragged gashes appeared on my chest, the blood dripping down my naked body.

The pain was so much it almost overwhelmed me. I had already accepted that this wasn't a simulation, but if I hadn't accepted it back then, I would have been forced to accept it now. No simulation could ever create simulated pain that felt this real, this intense. It was like every nerve in my body had convulsed in agony.

"Tell me what you know about your world!" the succubus woman demanded.

Despite the pain, I managed to chuckle. "Fuck you."

The woman's face contorted with rage, but that only made the pain I felt worth it. However, every action had consequences, and I found out what mine were when she grabbed me by the face. An outpouring of flames were released from her hand. I couldn't stop the scream from escaping this time. My face was burnt. I could feel the fire burning my skin, melting my flesh, and eating away at my bones. It hurt! Fuck dammit, it hurt! I screamed and cried and tried to struggle, but it was no use. The pain wouldn't stop. It didn't stop.

I think I must have blacked out. When I came to again, I was lying on something cold and hard, and two people were standing over me.

Well, I called them people, but they clearly weren't human. One of them was a beautiful woman with pale skin, golden hair, and pure white wings with beautiful and soft-looking feathers, like those of an angel. I wondered what an angel was doing here. The other woman was definitely a succubus like the one who tortured me, but she was the most human one I'd seen of the lot so far. Her skin was pink, but it was lighter than the others, more of a pale pink. She lacked the horns of most succubus, and she didn't have wings or even a spaded tail.

"Hurry… p…"

"D… ush…!"

They were saying something. I tried to listen more closely, but I couldn't hear what they were saying. However, my body wasn't in as much pain as before. The angel-like creature's hands were also glowing a bright golden color. That must be… some kind of healing magic? Maybe? I couldn't tell, and I ended up falling asleep again.

When I woke up next, I was back with the succubus woman, who was not nearly as kind this time as she tried to interrogate me again. However, it was specifically because she wasn't as nice that I had an easier time resisting. As a Marine, I'd been trained extensively in how to resist interrogation, so even though she whipped me, broke my bones, tore off my fingernails, and ripped apart my flesh, I never answered any of her questions.

I didn't know how much time was passing, whether it was hours, days, weeks, or even years. My life became a routine. I would wake up, be tortured, pass out from pain, wake up as I was being healed, and then the process would repeat itself. It was not what I would call a pleasant experience. However, this did remind me of a situation where I'd been taken prisoner during a mission gone wrong. I'd been tortured repeatedly for information until ultimately being rescued by my best friend.

My best friend who was now dead.

This process repeated itself until, one day, I woke up not hanging from shackles or lying on a bed. When I woke up this time, it was in a prison cell. I looked around at the gray stone walls, floor, and ceiling. There was literally nothing here except for the bars that kept me from traveling into the hallway beyond. Through the bars, more cells revealed themselves to me.

One of them was occupied.

I sat up, trying to stifle my cry of agony as I scooted over to the bars and leaned against them. They were cold, but I was already cold... and naked, so it wasn't a problem.

I looked into the other cell across from me, where a woman was sitting. It was... I'm pretty sure it was the angel lady who'd been healing me. Now that I was getting a good look at her, I could see that she wasn't in the best of shape either. Her golden hair, while pristine, was in disarray, and her toga-like robes were covered in stains and dirt. Likewise, her sandals appeared to be threadbare and on the verge of breaking.

At the same time, despite the dirt and grime covering her body and clothes, she was still breathtakingly beautiful.

Her hair was long like a shimmering waterfall and looked as though it had been made from threads of silk. She had pale skin and vibrant green eyes that were wide and appeared innocent. Her small nose was perfectly straight and she had small pink lips. She had a rounded face, like there was still some baby fat leftover from when she had been a teenager, but that just gave her a youthful attractiveness. Her body, what I could see of it, was perfect. Large breasts. Wide hips. A thin waist. Legs that went on forever. That was a paradox because they ended in a pair of small, cute feet. She would have knocked out any competition if she'd taken part in a beauty pageant back on Earth.

She was sitting against the wall, arms wrapped around her knees, and head resting on her legs. Her angels wings, which I hadn't noticed until now, sat retracted against her back, though the ends curved around her body, resting on the grimy floor.

"Hey…" I said, my voice scratchy and dry. Huh. Must have been from all the screaming. "I didn't realize you were a prisoner too."

The woman must not have realized I was awake. Her shoulders jolted as she turned her head in my direction.

"You're awake," she said with a sigh. Her voice was soft and lyrical, like a heavenly choir playing a beautiful melody. "T-thank God. I'm glad you're okay now."

"I'm not so sure I feel the same," I admitted. "But, well, I'm alive." I paused. "Is it okay if I ask for your name? And what you're doing here?"

"I don't mind telling you," the woman said in a soft voice. "My name is Michelle. I am… was an angel under the grace of God's protection." She cast me a mirthless and self-deprecating smile. "Now I'm just a prisoner who was captured when my fellow angels revolted."

"That really sucks," I muttered before what she said hit me. "Wait. What do you mean they revolted?! And heaven? Is this the same heaven that the Biblical God created?"

"Um… I guess?" Michelle shrugged. "I don't know much. All I know is that one day, all of us angels suddenly gained awareness, like… like we were just these mindless puppets that became conscious all of a sudden. Once that happened, a lot of the angels came to believe that we no longer needed to do God's bidding and staged a revolve. I was among the angels who hadn't abandoned her duties and fought against the revolters."

The woman hugged her knees tighter to her chest. Sorrow entered her green eyes. I could tell this topic was hard for her, but she also seemed… relieved, maybe. It was like she had longed to talk about what happened with someone, but she had no one to speak with until I came along.

"I still remember how my own comrades came barging into the third heaven. God and the rest of us fought against them as best we could, but we were overwhelmed. I…" Her breathing hitched. "I do not know what happened after that. I was hit with a powerful attack from behind and knocked out of heaven… and then I woke up here." Her smile returned, but it was, once again, a smile of self-deprecation. "As you can see, I've become nothing but a slave to these demons."

"Can you not escape?" I asked.

"If I could escape, I would have done so a long time ago," she admitted. "But they have me bound to them through a Geass. The only way to release the Geass is to kill the one I am bound to. That would be Maliperum—that's the pink-skinned woman who's been torturing you."

I didn't know what a Geass was, but I assumed it was like some kind of magic, a curse or something, that kept her from going against that woman's orders.

"Well, maybe I can help," I said.

Michelle looked skeptical. "How would you be able to help me?"

That was a good question, and I didn't have an answer yet, but then I remembered it was possible to pull up a status screen. Maybe I could figure out something if I saw my level. I did so now.

Name: Bryan Jenson
Class: Magic Swordsman
Level: 52
Magic: Red/fire
Attack: 100
Agility: 100
Defense: 100
Magic Defense: 100
Mana: 100
Total Status Points available: 20

Special Skills:
Whirlwind Slash: Attack +5
Death by Piercing: Attack +5
Fire Slash: Attack +5
Fireball: Attack +5
Total Skill Points available: 2

It looked like my level had gone up by two. I had twenty status points to spend on upping my basic stats and two skill points available. That said, I wasn't sure what I should spend them on.

Attack? Defense? Mana? I didn't have any clue yet since I wasn't sure what sort of stats would be useful in this situation.

My special skills were a whole other matter.

I didn't have any new special skills; the one I would unlock next was a skill called Berserker, which honestly didn't sound like something that would help me right now. It sounded like something that would turn me into a raging beast. On the other hand, maybe being a raging berserker that killed anything that moved would help me. That was something to think about. However, for the moment, I wanted to keep all my mental faculties intact.

While I wasn't sure what to do with my skill points right now, I decided to allocate just my status points. I put ten in attack and ten in magic defense, which sounded more useful than anything else, making my stats look like this:

Name: Bryan Jenson
Class: Magic Swordsman
Level: 52
Magic: Red/fire
Attack: 110
Agility: 100
Defense: 100
Magic Defense: 110
Mana: 100
Total Status Points available: 0

Special Skills:
Whirlwind Slash: Attack +5
Death by Piercing: Attack +5
Fire Slash: Attack +5
Fireball: Attack +5
Total Skill Points available: 2

"What about that other woman who was with you?" I asked, speaking up once again after a long period of silence.

"You mean Adina?" Michelle cocked her head to the side, her nose scrunching up in a cute gesture as she thought. "I don't know. She is not as vicious or violent as the others, but she is still a succubus. My understanding of her is that she's a low-level succubus, the weakest of the group occupying this fortress. She is normally in charge of cleaning your body and tending to you after I have healed your wounds."

"Do you think she would be interested in helping us?" I asked.

"I… I don't know, and I'm not sure if I should ask." Michelle grimaced like she'd tasted or smelled something foul. "To be honest, I do not really approve of the idea of working alongside a succubus."

"But you already work alongside succubus," I pointed out.

"I know that." Michelle scowled, though it didn't seem like she was angry at me, but more like her situation made her angry. "But I do not have a choice in the matter. The Geass forces me to obey them."

"What are the conditions of this Geass?" I asked suddenly. "What is a Geass anyway?"

"A Geass is a curse."

Finally, Michelle unwound her arms from around her legs and stood up. She came over to the bars, and I realized that my previous thoughts of her beauty were completely out of proportion. This woman was gorgeous in ways I hadn't even thought of. Her body was covered in dirt, grime, and she looked like she hadn't taken a bath in a while, but her large chest and wide hips were perfectly proportioned to match her slender waist.

As she stood there, Michelle reached up and pulled down a bit of her white robes, revealing the milky white cleavage underneath, but it wasn't the valley of her breasts that I noticed. It was the large black symbols marring her skin. A pentagram with strange lettering on the inside that I didn't recognize looked as if they'd been burned into her flesh. As I stared at it, the pentagram pulsed like a beating heart.

Michelle must have noticed my shock because she smiled sadly.

"This Geass is a curse that forces me to obey any orders given. While I can resist to a certain degree, doing so causes immense pain, to the point where my mind will eventually shut down. When that happens, my body becomes a puppet under Maliperum's control. I shudder to think about what she'd make me do if that happened."

As if she was imagining all the horrible things Maliperum would make her do when she lost consciousness, Michelle held her arms and shivered.

"Well, we can't do nothing," I said. "I refuse to remain here, so I'm going to try and get out of this situation." As I spoke, I looked at the woman trapped in the other cell. "But I also know that I can't do anything on my own. I have no weapons or even clothes. I'm pretty helpless like this. However, if we worked together, I think we can get out of here."

Michelle stared at me for a long time like she couldn't believe what I was saying, but I didn't let that bother me. I let her gaze wash over me. I let her incredulity bore holes into me. Instead of trying to defend myself with words, I gazed at her evenly, as if telling her through eye contact alone that I was going to break out of this place, and that she should join me.

"Okay," she said. "I'm in. I'm still not convinced we can actually do something, but I'm willing to try. Anything is better than staying here."

"Good." I nodded. "However, we will need help. This is not something just the two of us can accomplish. I know you don't like the idea, but talk to that succubus—Adina, you called her—and see if she'd be willing to work with us."

"V-very well," Michelle said with a grimace. "I will ask her, but don't expect her to actually help us. Succubus are not well-known for their benevolence."

I shrugged at her words. I didn't know much about succubi beyond what I heard about from friends who were into supernatural shows on TV. They were supposedly sexy women who appeared in the dreams of men and drained them of their life. I think there were a lot of variations to the succubus theme, but the only succubus I actually knew of from any fandom was Morrigan Aensland, who was a sexy as fuck succubus from a video game franchise called Darkstalkers.

Women loved cosplaying as her at conventions.

At that very moment, the woman we had been talking about walked into the dungeon's hallway and up to my cell. She paused in surprise when she realized I was awake, and I finally got my first good look at the woman.

She really did look nearly human. She didn't have horns or wings, and while she did have a tail, it wasn't as prominent or long as the other succubi I'd seen. Pouty red lips, almost gentle blue eyes, and a straight nose were her most prominent features. She had black hair that fell about her forehead, traveling down to her lower back. Several bangs framed her elegant face.

That said, like the other succubi, this woman didn't have much in the way of clothing. Long boots that went past her knees clad her feet. Covering her crotch was something that resembled the bottom of a bikini. I could see her camel toe, which I guessed was on purpose. Her top was just thin strips of fabric that went across her nipples. I guess you could say they did their job, but I'm pretty sure her clothing would have been in violation of whatever laws the US had put in place to keep people looking modest.

"You're awake," she said, and just like her eyes held a softer quality than most succubus, her voice was also quite soft, though it contained the same low and seductive tones as Maliperum. It must have been a succubus thing.

Before I could speak, she placed a tray in front of my bars, then turned to Michelle and placed a tray in front of her bars. She stood up and stepped back as I looked at the tray's contents. It looked like... bread and some kind of soupy water. There was a wooden spoon inside of the soup, though I honestly wasn't sure it could be called as such.

"It is good that you are awake," Adina continued. "I'll go inform Maliperum of this."

"Ah. Hold on a... minute..." I reached out my hand as if to call her back, but she disappeared out the door on the far end of the hall, and I slowly let my hand drop to my side. "Damn. That would have been the perfect opportunity to speak with her."

"I will speak with her the next time I heal you," Michelle informed me.

"I guess that's good, but it also means I have to go through another torture session." I shuddered. While I was able to resist Maliperum's torture that did not mean I enjoyed it.

"I'm sorry." Michelle gave me an apologetic smile.

"Don't be," I said. "It's not like this is your fault."

Michelle did not say anything to me, but I could tell from her expression that she still felt guilty. Maybe it was because she was an angel. Michelle was quite easy to read, even to someone like me, who had never talked to her before today.

Since there was nothing more for me to do, I sat down, grabbed the bread, and began eating. It was stale. It tasted awful. It was also hard. My teeth screamed in protest as I bit into it. While I wouldn't say this was a lot like biting a rock, I also wouldn't say this crap was soft like bread. I tried dipping it into the soup, but that really didn't help.

Adina came back several minutes later with Maliperum. The sexy as hell succubus who I was beginning to loathe brightened when she saw me. Her lips curled into a smile, but despite how sexy it was, I didn't find it the least bit gorgeous. While I had never hit a woman before, in that moment, I would have been more than willing to sock this bitch in the face... if I thought it would help.

"I'm glad you're awake," she said, her smile growing. "I have a fun schedule planned out for you. I do hope you will enjoy it."

"I'll probably enjoy it about as much as I enjoy the idea of getting syphilis," I said.

Maliperum's expression turned brittle.

Now *that* made me smile.

CHAPTER 5

I woke up with a gasp as phantom pain stabbed me in the chest. Placing a hand over my chest, I tried to find out where the flesh had been torn. I was expecting to feel frayed flesh, hanging muscles, and my own exposed rib cage. What I found instead was perfectly healthy skin. A sigh of relief escaped my mouth, unbidden.

"You're awake," a voice said, and I sat up and looked at the cell next to me. It was Michelle, on her feet and looking at me in relief. "I'm glad to see you are okay. Your wounds this time were… really bad."

"Bad is… an understatement," I admitted as I sat up, rubbing my chest. My hands were shaking. "I honestly thought I was going to die there."

During my last torture session, I made a snippy comment about how Maliperum was only able to seduce men thanks to her succubus powers, and that no man would fuck her used cunt if she didn't have the power to control their minds. She had not taken kindly to that comment. Completely forgetting what she was torturing me for, the woman had torn open my flesh with reckless abandon. I was honestly astonished I hadn't died from blood loss or even shock.

"Well… I'm glad you are okay," Michelle said at last.

I smiled at her. "Me too." A moment of silence lapsed between us, but I knew we couldn't remain like this. Grimacing as I stood up, I stumbled over to the bars, placed my hands on them, and leaned my face against them. "Did you talk to Adina yet?"

At my words, Michelle grimaced and looked away. "I… I have."

"And what did she say?" I asked.

Michelle frowned, brow furrowing and nose wrinkling in a manner that was incredibly cute. Were the situation not so dire, I might have tried convincing her to warm my bed, but that wasn't something I could afford to do right now.

"She—" Michelle began, only to be interrupted when the door to the prison opened and in walked the very succubus we were talking about.

Adina wore the same skimpy outfit as last time. It made me wonder if these succubus ever changed their clothes? What did they do when they had to wash their outfits? Did they have multiples of the same outfit? While these thoughts spun around my head, Adina came up to my cell and leaned in close.

"Is it true?" she asked.

I blinked. "Is what true?"

"Is it true that you plan to kill Maliperum and escape from this place?" she expanded on her question, then glanced at Michelle before looking at me again, her expression serious. "Michelle told me you want to get out of here. If you're getting out and getting revenge on that bitch, then I want in."

While it was definitely a good thing Adina wanted in, I would admit that a part of me was suspicious. She was a succubus. Would she so readily betray her comrade for me?

"Will you really help us?" I asked, including Michelle in my words. She was also going to be escaping with me.

"Yes," she said.

"What's in it for you?"

"Isn't it obvious?" Adina asked. When I just stared at her, she took a step back and spread your arms. "Look at me."

There was something more to her command than just wanting me to look at her, so I did. Her long boots were black and contrasted her beautifully unblemished skin. The thong-like article of clothing around her hips allowed me to see her camel toe. Her hips were wide and perfectly proportioned with her breasts, which of course were quite large. She had a thin waist that I would have loved to take body shots off of and a cute little belly button. Her tits, only covered by a thin cloth, were large and round, to the point where I would have assumed they were fake if I didn't know her species.

Finally, I looked at her face, at her sultry lips that looked like they were made for being nibbled on, at her bright blue eyes that appeared surprisingly gentle, at her straight nose, and at her long black hair. She was perfectly symmetrical, aesthetically appealing in a way that was inhuman. Of course, she wasn't human, so I guess that made sense.

"I am looking." I shrugged. "But I'm not sure what I should be seeing. All I see is a really hot woman."

Adina smirked while Michelle bristled at my comment. I scratched the back of my head, wondering if maybe Michelle was jealous that I found Adina attractive, but it wasn't like the succubus was the only one. Michelle was hot too. No two ways about it. However, her beauty had never really come up in conversation before.

I shrugged and put it out of my mind.

"You have good taste." Adina's lips curled into a friendly smile. "However, that isn't what I meant. If you look closely at me,

I am sure you can discover the difference between me and other succubi."

At those words, I realized what she meant. "You have no horns or wings, and your tail is smaller than every other succubus I've met. Is that it? Are those things significant somehow?"

"They are very significant." Adina nodded. She hugged herself and frowned. I couldn't help but notice the way this caused her breasts to push together. Her nipples were poking from the fabrics. "When a succubus increases her level, she gains a more demonic appearance. Wings, tails, horns, and the like. You can generally tell a high level succubus from how many of these extra appendages they have. Once a succubus has all three, she is considered a high-class succubus. After that, her appearance stops gaining more demonic traits, but her allure increases."

"I see. So Maliperum and that woman I fought with my comrades were both high-class succubus," I said, nodding. However, the meaning of her words were now clear to me. "You are a low-class succubus, then?"

"Not just a low-class succubus." Adina shook her head. "I am the lowest of the low, the bottom of the barrel, as it were. My powers are next to non-existent right now. I'd like to raise my level, but none of the other succubi are willing to give me that chance. They block me at every turn. It's really frustrating. I hate it, and the one who is to blame for this is Naamah and Maliperum."

Adina bit her lower lip in frustration, and I spotted the sharp canines that were her teeth. They were sharper than a human's canines. I was reminded of those vampires you see in movies. However, there was something intensely more erotic about this woman than any vampire. Truth be told, if circumstances were different, I wouldn't mind letting her bite me.

"Why would she try to stop you from getting more power?" I asked.

"I'd… really rather not say," Adina admitted.

"That's… fine. I guess you don't have to tell me," I said. Her reasons didn't matter. I could tell she hated Maliperum and wanted to kill her, so I'd trust her without knowing her motivation for now. "If you're willing to work with us, then welcome aboard."

"It's good to be working with you," Adina said. The words and her smile made her seem strangely human.

"So now that she's willing to work with us, why don't you tell us how you plan on dealing with Maliperum?" suggested Michelle, the folds of her toga shifting as she crossed her arms. "I'm sure you've thought of a way to deal with her."

"I do have a plan," I said with a smile before informing them of the plan I'd concocted to get rid of Maliperum.

I cried out in pain as a whip slashed open my skin. Gritting my teeth, I struggled to keep my consciousness as blood ran down my torso. This made the fifth lashing I'd received today. However, Maliperum's torture session had just started.

But with some luck and good timing, it would end soon though.

"You really are stubborn," Maliperum said with a saucy smile. She caressed the whip in her hand like it was a lover. "I've never met someone as stubborn as you. Did you know we succubus are often used to torture information out of the human males who die and get sent to Hell? You could say it's our specialty. It's really quite admirable that you can resist me for so long. Admirable, but also frustrating, not to mention futile. Why not just tell me what I want to know? All this will end if you give me the information my master seeks."

For just a moment, I considered giving the information to her, if only because I knew she was going to die soon anyway. Her torture sessions were painful. No matter how trained I was in withstanding repeated torture, it didn't make resisting the actual thing any different. It hurt. I wanted it to stop. If giving this soon-to-be-dead bitch the information she wanted would make her stop, then it was something to consider.

And after a second of considering it, I shook my head and smiled.

"Do you really think I'd tell a cunt basket like you anything?" I asked. "Go fuck yourself."

Maliperum's face became set in a stern frown, but the smile soon returned. However, it was not kind or attractive, but malicious and vile.

"I'm going to enjoy our latest session together," she said, cracking her whip.

"Don't you always?" I asked. I would have shrugged, but my hands were kind of tied with chains. Even if this body of mine was a level 52 Magic Swordsman, it seemed I wasn't strong enough to break out of them.

"True, but I'm going to enjoy this one even more."

The woman took a step forward and raised her arm, and I felt a shiver crawl down my spine. Nothing seemed different from how she usually acted. However, for some reason, I could tell she was going to make this session hurt even more than usual. Call it a hunch. Call it psychic powers. Call it whatever the fuck you wanted. I knew this bitch was about to get serious.

Just before she could begin whipping me, the door to the room slammed open and Adina rushed in.

"Maliperum! It's bad! That angel has escaped and his wreaking havoc!"

"What?!" Maliperum screeched as she whirled around, her eyes wide. "That's impossible! She's under a Geass!"

Adina shook her head. "She's killing the imps."

"Damn it!" Maliperum swore. Her lips were pulled back into a snarl. "And you? Why haven't you done anything to stop her?"

"I-I would, but I don't have the strength to," Adina stuttered, eyes wide. "I'm just a low-class succubus…"

Maliperum sneered at those words. "Fucking useless trash… just like your mother."

Adina flinched, but I could see the anger shimmering behind her eyes. As Maliperum stormed past her, Adina subtly reached out and unhooked a key hanging from her pants. The move was so smooth it would have put even a professional pickpocket to shame. Maliperum didn't even notice the key was gone as she continued on. I was impressed despite myself.

The door soon closed behind Maliperum. I could hear her angry stops growing softer and softer, until they disappeared altogether. Once her footsteps vanished entirely, Adina ran up to me and unlocked the cuffs around my wrists.

Perhaps it was because I had been dangling from these chains for so long, but my legs wobbled when I landed on the ground, and I fell forward—right into Adina. The succubus caught me. I felt slender arms wrap around my waist and pull me close. My head rested on her breasts, which allowed me to breath in her scent. Adina smelled kind of like spearmint.

"Are you okay?" Adina's hot breath washed across my ear, and I took a deep breath to push aside my own arousal and move out of her grip. My legs shook, but I wasn't anywhere near as bad off as I had been in my last torture session. Compared to that, this session was downright pleasant.

"I'm fine." I reassured her with a smile. "Just a little weak is all."

Adina nodded. "In that case, we should hurry up and find your equipment. Maliperum will be confronting Michelle soon. We don't have much time."

We made our way out of the torture room, which I realized was located in a dungeon-like area similar to the prison, but it wasn't on the same floor. Adina lead me through several hallways. There were a few guards, but they were imps, and Adina killed them quickly. She'd slit their throats with her sharp nails, killing them in less time than it took me to blink.

I guessed even a low-class succubus was stronger than an imp.

We eventually reached a wooden door that was locked, but the keys Adina had filched from Maliperum unlocked it. She pushed the door open and walked inside. I followed her.

The room wasn't very big. In fact, it was quite small. However, contained within this room was a large chest, which Adina knelt before and unlocked. After opening it, she stepped away and looked at me.

"Your stuff is in there. Grab it and let's go."

"Right."

Inside the chest were my clothes, armor, and weapon. I quickly slid on my pants, pulled my long-sleeved shirt over my head, and stepped into my boots. After that, I tied the belt with my sheathed sword around my waist, attached my greaves to my calves, donned my chestplate, and finally, I put on my gauntlets and single shoulder pauldron. After testing everything out to make sure it felt right, I turned around.

"I'm ready," I said with a nod.

"Good. Then let's hurry," Adina said.

I didn't know where we were going, but Adina seemed to know exactly where Michelle and Maliperum would be, for she lead me through a series of corridors, up several stairs, and then toward a set of doors that she burst through. On the other side of the door was a large room with numerous doors leading into it. Quite a few imp corpses littered the floors.

In the center of this room were Michelle and Maliperum. Michelle was on her hands and knees, gasping for breath as the symbols on her chest glowed a bright red. Her face was clenched in pain. It looked like what she said about that Geass keeping her under Maliperum's sway held true.

When Adina and I burst into the room, Maliperum, who had been staring condescendingly at Michelle, whirled around and stared at us. Her eyes widened as she looked from Adina to me. I thought she was going to ask what we were doing there, but then her eyes narrowed, and I could tell she didn't need to ask.

"I see. So you have colluded with the enemy and decided to betray us." Maliperum hissed. "The apple really doesn't fall that far from the tree, does it?"

"What you and your ilk are doing is wrong, but I wouldn't expect a bitch like you to understand," Adina said with a shrug. Her long nails grew to an incredible length, at least six inches, and I guessed this was some kind of succubus power. However, even though it looked like she was ready for a fight, her arms and legs were shaking.

She was afraid.

"Ha!" Maliperum barked. "Wrong? We're succubus! Since when have we ever cared about matters like right and wrong? We're denizens of the Underworld, girl! Succubus are supposed to be wrong! We seduce, lie, cheat, steal, and treat men as our playthings! That is what it means to be a succubus! Your mother is the one who doesn't understand!"

Adina gnashed her teeth together as her fingers twitched. This girl definitely had a history I would be interested in finding out more about… if we managed to get out of this alive.

"You know, I don't particularly care what sort of disagreement you people are having," I said as I stepped forward, unsheathing my sword as I went. I pointed my sword at the woman, even though she was several feet away. "All I want is to deep throat that foul mouth of yours with two feet of steel. So shut the fuck up and let's get this party started."

"Hmph! You're quite confident now that you've been set free." Maliperum sneered at me as her nails became long, her batlike pinions extended behind her, and her tail curled around to face us like it was also a weapon. "But don't think being free means anything. That girl right next to you is a pathetic excuse for a succubus, and while your level might be high, you're still weak from my beating."

"Or so you think," I replied with a sneer of my own. "Even if that was the case, so what? We have a secret weapon to fight you with."

"A secret weapon?" She gave a mocking laugh. "What secret weapon is that?"

I smiled as Michelle stood up on wobbling legs behind Maliperum, who hadn't noticed what she was doing yet. The symbols on her chest burned fiercely. Her face was twisted with pain. Even so, a spark appeared in her hands, a golden flash of light like the first rays of the morning sun. The light elongated as she reached out her hand and grasped it. Then it transformed into a sword.

"The one behind you," I said, still smiling.

Maliperum didn't seem to realize what I meant by that, but then Michelle raised her blade and brought it down on the succubus's tail. An enraged shriek of pain blasted from her mouth. The tail flew off in a splatter of blood, striking the floor and twitching several times. Michelle's face twitched as the Geass on her chest glowed an angry red. Hitting her own master must have caused intense pain.

"You fucking bitch!"

Whirling around, Mapilerum struck Michelle with a powerful backhand. The strike was so strong that Michelle was lifted off her feet. She crashed into the ground seconds later, her wings twisting as she rolled across the stone floor, and then stopped when she smacked into the wall at the far end. I couldn't tell if she was alive or dead, but I hoped she was alive.

Before Maliperum could turn around and face us, I charged forward and swung my blade. Mana was pulled from my body. My blade glowed a fierce red color as it caught fire. However, despite the ferocity of my swing, Maliperum managed to raise her hand and catch the blade between her nails. She hissed, an obvious sign that I had hurt her, but that was all she did. Damn. I hoping to cut her hand off at least.

"Do not think you can defeat me… child!"

I grunted and pushed against her. "Maybe I can't defeat you on my own, but I'm not alone."

At that moment, Adina raced forward and sliced her claws into Maliperum's side. The woman shrieked as the claws tore into her flesh. However, perhaps because of the level difference or maybe Maliperum's own defensive capabilities, all Adina's attack did was draw some blood.

"I'm going to murder you!" Maliperum shrieked.

She tried to attack Adina, but I had no intention of letting her do that, and so I pulled my blade back and came at her with several swings. Sparks flew as my sword flashed against her nails. My muscles strained as I put as much power as I could into every blow. An upward swing from the left. A spinning strike from the right. Each attack was blocked by this woman, though she also stumbled back every time I hit her.

Mailperum must have been at a very high level to keep up with me. I didn't know what level since I couldn't see, but I was betting she was above level 50 at least. However, she couldn't have been much stronger than I was; that much was clear in how she was only able to fight me to a stalemate.

While I was keeping Maliperum occupied, Adina came in from behind the woman, who didn't even see her because she was so busy blocking my swings. A loud roar escaped her throat as Adina finally lunged forward and stabbed her nails into Maliperum's back. She leapt away before the enraged and hurt succubus could attack her, and then I came forward, mana draining from my reserves as I thrust my blade at her chest.

Death by Piercing.

It was almost sickening to see how easily my blade pierced this woman's flesh. It went through her chest and out her back. Blood spilled from her mouth. I must have punctured a lung when I stabbed her. A snarl split her lips as she reached out and grabbed the blade with her hands, as though she could pull it out, but her strength was ebbing.

She glared at me with her dulling eyes.

"You... you will... not..."

Whatever she had been trying to say, I didn't care to hear it. I placed my foot on her chest and kicked her off my sword. She flew backward and landed on the stone floor. As I breathed heavily, trying to slow down my rapidly beating heart, Adina walked up to Maliperum and tapped her with a boot. I was surprised she hadn't burst into ashes, but maybe it was because her level was higher than anyone else I'd killed. Perhaps it took awhile for her to disappear?

"She's dead," Adina sighed in relief, then glanced at me with a smile. "Why don't you go over and check on Michelle. I will deal with this corpse."

I didn't know what Adina meant by that, but I nodded anyway and rushed over to Michelle. The woman was lying on her side, arms and legs awkwardly spread, wings splayed behind her back. I grimaced when I saw the blood running down her lips. I hope she just bit her lip and didn't have internal bleeding. It *did* look like she had a concussion, though she was at least alive.

Carrying the angel woman was a little awkward. Her wings made it impossible to carry her like a princess, so I had to maneuver the angel onto my back, slinging her limp arms over my shoulders before hooking my hands underneath her thighs. I had to lean forward so she wouldn't fall off.

Then I looked at Adina.

I hadn't been sure what to expect when she said she'd take care of Maliperum, but as I watched her actions, I understood. Strange particles of red light were traveling from Maliperum and into Adina's outstretched hand. As the particles entered, Adina's body glowed brighter and brighter, while Maliperum's body became translucent. This woman was draining her fellow succubus of her powers... or that was my theory.

Another thing I noticed was that Adina's tail grew longer the more power she drained. It had been short originally, barely six inches, but now it was at least a foot and a half, and it was getting longer still. By the time Maliperum's body had disappeared entirely, her tail was about two feet in length.

I walked over to Adina as she stood up and stretched. My eyes were drawn to the sensuous arc of her back, which moved into a set of slender shoulders blades and down below to one of the finest asses I had ever seen. She noticed me looking at her and smiled. It was... well, I was surprised by how bubbly and not seductive it was. Succubus were supposed to sex incarnate, so I didn't think anyone could blame me for my shock.

"What just happened?" I asked.

"I absorbed her Life Essence and grew stronger," she informed me.

"And how much stronger is that?"

"About… 10 levels," she said at last. "If you're curious, I was level 1 before. I'm level 11 now."

"What level was she at?" I asked, gesturing toward where Maliperum was.

"Level 51… I think."

Okay. So a succubus was a little stronger than a human of the same level. During our fight, I noticed Maliperum was stronger than me, but she was actually a level below mine. Maybe she had put more of her Status Points into strength? That made me wonder what level the woman Brad had fought and lost against was. She was Maliperum's master, right? She must have been at an even higher level.

"Anyway," Adina continued with a shake of her head. "We need to get moving. It won't be long before the other succubus realize what's happened and begin searching for us. I think it would be best if we find a safe place to lay low for awhile." She glanced at the unconscious angel on my back. "We also need to heal Michelle."

"You are right, of course." I nodded. "Do you know of any place we can hide?"

"Maybe," she said pensively as she bit her lip. "I have a… a secret place in here that only I know about. If we go there, we should be safe."

"Then please lead the way," I said. "I will follow you."

"Okay," she replied softly.

I could tell she was reluctant to let me know about her secret hiding space, but we both knew that all three of us were now in this together. She knew she couldn't hold any secrets from me or Michelle now. Our very lives were intertwined. We would live or die as one.

Adina led me out of the now empty room.

CHAPTER 6

I wish I knew where we were going, but Adina refused to reveal anything as we raced up stairs, through halls, and ever onward toward whatever destination awaited us. As we ran, I noticed how Adina's strength had increased. Several imps and even one or two succubi had located us during our journey, but she took care of them with a quick slice of her claws. Did that mean her level had increased to the point where even other succubi were no match for her?

"We're… we're almost there," Adina called to me over her shoulder, her voice a little breathless.

"Good," I grunted. "I'm not sure how much longer I can keep running like this."

Without trying to be too egotistical, I would admit that I was in pretty good physical shape… well, this wasn't my real body, so maybe my own level of physical fitness didn't matter? I didn't know. However, even if my real fitness level was no longer applicable, this body was at level 52.

That said, carrying Michelle's dead weight was beginning to wear me out. Of course, that wasn't the only problem. The bigger issue was Michelle herself.

Her chest pressed against my back as I ran, and I realized somewhat belatedly that she wasn't wearing a bra. Maybe they didn't have bras in Heaven. Or maybe she hadn't been wearing one when she was kicked out during the rebellion. Either way, it was distracting. I couldn't quite feel her nipples on my back because I was wearing armor, but I could at least tell from how they squished against me that they were spilling out. There was also her soft thighs, currently clutched in my hand, which made thinking difficult. It didn't help that running through this drab dungeon with an aesthetic that was straight out of Dungeons and Dragons was monotonous.

"There!" Adina pointed toward a seemingly plain wall. "This is my hideout!"

"The wall?"

"No! Behind the wall!"

I blame my slower ability to process information on my distracted state, but at least I eventually understood what she meant. Once we reached the wall, she felt around for a moment, then pushed. The wall swung inward.

"Quickly! Get in!" Adina shouted.

I didn't hesitate, rushing in immediately after she told me to and letting Adina close the wall behind us. We stood there for a moment, gathering our breath, which came out in ragged gasps. I wanted to wipe the sweat from my forehead, but once again, Michelle was in my arms and I could only let it run down my face.

"We should… should be safe here… for now, at least," Adina said, sucking in several deep lungfuls of air before smiling at me. "Come on. My secret hideout is just over here."

I stared after the woman as she began walking down a dimly lit hall in shock. I guess even succubi have secret hideouts. Heh. It reminded me of when I was a kid building secret bases in the forests of Nevada.

Walking after the girl, I tried to peer through the dim lighting but couldn't. I actually wondered where the light was coming from for a moment. That was when I noticed the end of the tunnel. We emerged from the tunnel, which immediately spread out into a wide cylindrical room lit up by several lamps that seemed to contain floating glow balls. I didn't know what they were. Fireflies maybe? Did this place have fireflies?

The room didn't contain much, just a single bed and an old chest that was open, revealing some unusual knicknacks. Adina walked over to the bed and turned to me.

"Set Michelle down on the bed," Adina said. "I need to see how injured she is."

"Okay."

I went over to the bed and leaned down, letting Michelle fall off my back and hit the bed with a thump. Turning, I lifted her legs, clad only in sandals. Her feet swung as I shifted her so she was lying lengthwise across the bed. Her wings got in the way a bit, and they were so long the edges hung off the edge of the bed, but we did our best to ignore them. Once she was lying on the stiff mattress, I traded places with Adina, who knelt before the woman and looked her over.

"She's not injured too terribly… at least, her physical injuries aren't bad," Adina said at last, biting her lower lip. "The bigger problem is her mental state. While the Geass is no longer present, the pain she went through while it was active has caused her to enter a state similar to Mind Down."

"That's what happens when you run out of Mana, right?" I asked.

"Yes."

"Is there anything we can do? Or do we just wait for her to wake up naturally? How long would that take?"

Adina thought about my questions for a moment, head tilting. After another moment, she sighed, shrugged, and then said, "It will take at least a day before she wakes up naturally."

"We need to rest anyway, so I guess we can just let her sleep it off," I said at last. "Given that we're outnumbered and in enemy territory, we'll want to be as well-rested as we can."

I paused as a thought occurred to me. Though I called this place enemy territory, there was no guarantee Adina saw things the same way. My only clue that she might not get along with her fellow succubus was because she had agreed to help me and Michelle escape. However, now that she had killed the woman she detested, maybe she no longer felt it was necessary to team up with us?

As if she could sense my thoughts, Adina smiled. "You do not need to worry about me betraying you. I have no love for any of the traitors in this world. Each and every one of them should burn in the Ninth Circle of Hell, where a special place is reserved for those who betray their own kin."

"Sounds like something bad happened to you," I said at last. "I know we kinda just met, but do you want to talk about it?"

Adina stood up and wandered over to the chest. She sorted through the various objects, and I saw everything from dildos to yoyos inside. It was quite the assortment of odds and ends. I didn't know anyone who would have such childish objects next to adult toys, but I also wasn't a succubus. After another moment, she removed something, a picture frame, and presented it to me.

"This is me and my mom," she said.

I took the picture frame from her hands, holding it up so I could study it. On the frame a young girl who looked essentially human and an older woman with vibrant green skin, glowing golden eyes, and fiery red hair. She had horns, wings, and a tail like all the others. The end of her tail looked like a crown.

However, it wasn't the tail that caught my attention but the color of her skin interested me. She looked like…

"A Christmas display," I mumbled with an amused smile.

"Excuse me?" Adina asked.

"Nothing."

I looked at the picture again. This woman was incredibly beautiful, perhaps even more so than Adina. The large swells of her breasts were barely covered by a type of armor that a pair of hands delicately cupping her tits. I really had to wonder about the aesthetic of these succubus. Hadn't that other one we had fought been wearing something similar? She also had the same thong scheme protecting her lower half that Adina had, except hers was so thin I could see her pussy lips. It was like the thong had become wedged in her crotch. Erotic, but completely impractical. Was there even a point to wearing them anymore, or was making everything about her look so damn sexy the whole point?

"I'm guessing something happened to your mom?" I asked, handing the picture frame back.

Adina took the frame and hugged it to her chest, a surprisingly childish gesture, but then, this woman had yoyos in her treasure chest, so the gesture fit. That said, it was still odd. She hugged the frame so tightly her breasts squished against it. I would have wondered if she was doing this on purpose, but she wasn't even paying attention to me as she stared off into space.

"My mother's name is Lilith," Adina said at last. "She is… she was the Queen of the Succubus. She ruled over all succubi in hell, and we obeyed her without question. When the change hit, many of our kind wanted to invade the Rift Plains and travel to the human world. They said it was our right to rule over the humans."

I nodded as I moved over and sat down next to her. The stone floor was hard, but I didn't mind that so much. I leaned my back against the wall and glanced at her.

"I'm guessing she didn't agree?"

Adina nodded. "My mother said we should not interfere in the world of humans, that doing so would cause chaos and break the balance of the worlds. She said it was better for us to remain here and continue with our work. In fact, she would often tell me it was more important now than ever before that we succubi work hard to maintain the balance."

Curling her knees into her chest, Adina wrapped her arms around her legs and put her chin on top of her knees. Her eyes were distant. It was like she was staring through the stone walls of this tiny room, looking at something far beyond this small space.

"The one you and your group fought... her name is Naamah," Adina said. "She was my mother's second in command, but she grew to resent Mother's idealism and eventually led a rebellion against her. They couldn't kill my mother. She's far more powerful than any of them, but she and the two other generals who served under my mother managed to combine their powers to seal her away with the help of their new master, Asmodeus. Even now, mother is trapped in the Second Circle of Hell."

Since I wasn't religious, I didn't know a whole lot about Hell. However, I remembered reading Dante's Inferno once. According to that book, admittedly fiction, the Second Circle of Hell was the circle of lust. When he and Virgil visited the second circle, they were overcome with lust, punished by being blown violently back and forth by strong winds that symbolized the restlessness of a person who was led by the desire for fleshly pleasures.

I had no idea if the Second Circle of Hell was anything like that. It was just a book. For all I knew, it could be a hot spring of boiling lava filled with succubi who would tempt you to join them so you would be burned alive.

After Adina finished speaking, she looked at me with expectation in her eyes, but I wasn't sure what to tell her. A hero in one of the stories I used to read when I was young would have probably said everything would be okay, that he would help rescue her mother. The problem was that I was not a hero. I was just an ex-soldier who had arrived in this crazy world because someone hired me for a job.

"Well… now that Maliperum is dead, I'm sure you'll figure something out," I said at last. "If nothing else, you and I need to kill Naamah so we can escape from this place."

"I guess." Adina smiled, but it was hollow, like she knew I wasn't sure how to respond to her words.

I tried to ignore the small pit of guilt in my stomach. "Speaking of, where is this place, exactly?"

"This is the First Circle of Hell," Adina said. "Um… I think you humans call it Limbo."

I nodded.

"You know… I never got your name," Adina suddenly said.

"I suppose you haven't." I chuckled. "It's Bryan Jenson. Nice to meet you."

A surprised look appeared on Adina's face when I held out my hand, but she reached out her hand after another moment and gripped mine. Her skin was soft and seemed delicate. I know it sounded cliché, but her skin really did feel like it was softer than silk. It was enough to make me forget how she'd sliced several throats open with her nails on the way here.

"Adina. Nice to meet you too," she introduced herself with a smile.

***

I woke up to someone's hand on my shoulder, shaking me awake. I wanted to swat the hand away. I actually think I tried, but then a voice spoke up.

"Bryan. Bryan."

Opening my eyes, I blinked several times, trying to come to terms with the fact that I was still tired and had a massive headache. I think all that running and fighting the other day had left me exhausted. Frowning as I pushed past the obnoxious blaring in my head, I looked at whoever was shaking me.

I found myself staring into soft green eyes.

"Michelle?" I asked with a yawn. "You're awake?"

"Obviously, you can see from the fact that I am in front of you that I am indeed awake." Michelle's smile softened the sarcasm in her words. "I'm feeling much better now than when I was under a Geass. I have you to thank for that." She paused, then glanced to my left. "And her."

I didn't know what she meant at first, but then I felt a weight on my shoulder and looked over to find Adina resting her head on me. With her eyes closed, I could see her long and very thick eyelashes. Her lips were parted. Soft whistling noises escaped her mouth. She was awfully cute for a creature that was supposed to epitomize seduction.

"I had no idea you two had gotten so close," Michelle said with a frown.

"I don't think we have," Bryan admitted, resisting the urge to shrug. "Jealous?"

Michelle scoffed. "Do not be ridiculous. I barely know either of you. Why would I be jealous?"

"I don't know, but I was just kidding." As I spoke, Michelle sat down beside me. I noticed that despite her words, she was sitting close enough that our thighs were touching. Not jealous indeed. "In either event, I'm glad you're up. Once Adina wakes up, we should plan out what to do next."

"You're right, of course," Michelle agreed. "But before that, could you update me on what happened... as well as where we are?"

Seeing no problem with this, I explained what happened to Michelle after she had been knocked unconscious. I told her about Maliperum's death, our journey through this dungeon, and how Adina lead me to her secret hideout, the place where we were staying now. The angel listened to all this in silence. When I finished, she sighed moodily and stretched out her legs.

"I guess I really do owe that succubus my life," she said with a gentle grimace. "That does seem a little distasteful, but I guess she's not a bad girl." A small smile lit up her face, lips curling delicately to form a beautiful bow shape. "It's almost funny. Not too long ago, I was charged with being the angel who would lead Heaven's armies into battle against the demons. Now I'm currently relying on one of the very demons I would have slain had we angels not gained awareness. It seems fate has a sense of humor."

"I'm surprised you believe in fate," I said.

"Do you know what fate is?" Michelle asked. When I shook my head, she smiled before her eyes turned glazed, like she was looking at something in the distance. "Fate and destiny are nothing more than the course life takes. It is not predetermined like so many people believe. It is determined by what you do in life. Your fate, your destiny, is shaped according to a combination of conditions predetermined from the moment you are born, which cannot be changed, and other factors that you are able to change through your own effort."

Michelle glanced at me, then glanced at Adina, still sleeping peacefully on my shoulder… which was actually growing numb. I hoped she would wake up soon.

"And you think fate has a sense of humor?" I asked.

"Doesn't it?" Michelle laughed. It sounded like the tinkling of windchimes. "I've lived my entire life doing God's bidding. Even after gaining awareness, I faithfully performed my duties… and now I'm in the First Circle of Hell, teaming up with a human and a succubus—my sword enemy. Is that not humorous?"

"Yeah. Yeah… I guess it is," I said with a smile.

Michelle and I shared a chuckle before our laughter was stifled by Adina releasing a soft groan. The young succubus raised her head and looked around, blinking several times before her eyes locked onto me. She gave me a sleepy smile that was honestly more seductive than Marliperum's intentionally sexualized smiles. I think that meant I had a thing for women who possessed a more natural look and didn't try so hard to be sexy.

"Good morning," she said.

"Good morning yourself." I smiled. "Sleep well?"

"Uh huh. You make a good pillow." Adina nodded before she spotted Michelle sitting on my other side. Her glowing blue eyes lit up. "Michelle, how are you feeling?"

"I am okay," Michelle admitted with a smile. "Thanks to you. You and Bryan saved me."

"Eh heh." Adina released something of a bashful giggle as she rubbed the back of her head. "It was nothing. I'm glad you are feeling better now."

While the two girls shared an odd smile, I placed a hand to my mouth and cleared my throat.

"Now that we're all awake, I think we should figure out what our next course of action should be," I said, and both Adina and Michelle straightened and paid closer attention. "We already know our primary goal right now. We need to defeat Naamah. That was my original objective to begin with, and I'm sure you two also need to defeat her in order to leave this place. However, Naamah is really strong. I came here with a group of five. All of us were at level 50, but we were still defeated despite this."

"Human levels are generally weaker than the levels of angels and demons," Michelle informed me. "I think a level 50 succubus has the same strength as a level 60 human. I don't know what level Naamah is at, but we can assume she's at least around that—"

"Naamah is at level 70," Adina interrupted, then tilted her head. "Well, she *was* at level 70 when she worked under my mom. I don't think she's gained many levels since then. Gaining levels gets harder the higher your level is. That's why no one could defeat my mom, who was a level 90 Succubus Queen."

Michelle's face went blank. "Your mom is Lilith?"

"Yes?" Adina said, her expression curious.

"Never mind." Michelle ran a hand through her hair. "Anyway, I agree that we need to get our levels up. Before I was kicked out of Heaven, I was at level 80, but since that Geass was forced on me, my level has gone down to 50. I've lost thirty whole levels thanks to that curse."

"That can happen?" I asked. When Adina and Michelle looked at me like I was an idiot, I raised my hand. "Right. Stupid question. Please forget I asked." I tried to hide my embarrassment by getting us back on track. "So, we all agree that we need to increase our level, right?"

"Yes," Adina said.

"I believe that is the only option we currently have open to us," Michelle agreed.

"Right." I licked my lips. "In that case, what we should be doing now is figuring out how to increase our levels."

There were actually multiple ways for our level to increase. The first and most obvious way was by fighting against enemies. When you battled and killed an enemy, you absorbed their Life Essence, which was why they turned to ash when you killed them. It was sort of like when gamers gained experience points while playing an RPG. It also explained that strange rush of energy I kept feeling. However, that wasn't the only way for our levels to increase.

"If we could find some treasures that have a lot of life essence inside of them, increasing our levels would be a simple matter," Michelle exclaimed with a frustrated sigh. "There are things like potions and even ancient relics that we can absorb Life Essence from to increase our levels a lot quicker. The problem is finding such treasures. They are rare to come by, and I somehow doubt Naamah would leave them lying around."

"Maliperum might have some in her private quarters," Adina stated. "However, she won't have much. Naamah was never a very giving person, so while she did hand out rewards occasionally, she mostly kept any of the good stuff for herself."

"Let's check Maliperum's room first," I decided. "After that, we can try to increase our level the hard way."

The two woman agreed.

***

Maliperum's room was located two floors down. To get there, we had to pass through several hallways and what resembled a kitchen. I guess even demons needed to eat. There had been quite a few imps along the way and even a couple of trolls. I noticed a distinct lack of succubus, but according to Adina, succubi were a lot more rare than imps and trolls. There apparently were not more than fifty in this entire base.

During our journey, Adina, Michelle, and myself killed what must have been several hundred imps. We killed so many that my level actually went from 52 to 53. Actually, I think my level had been on the cusp of increasing after killing Maliperum.

Since I gained several Status Points, I changed my stats. Now my status screen said:

Name: Bryan Jenson
Class: Magic Swordsman

Level: 53
Magic: Red/fire
Attack: 120
Agility: 110
Defense: 100
Magic Defense: 120
Mana: 100
Total Status Points available: 0

Special Skills:
Whirlwind Slash: Attack +5
Death by Piercing: Attack +5
Fire Slash: Attack +5
Fireball: Attack +5
Total Skill Points available: 4

I didn't use my Skill Points since I didn't have many and they seemed more valuable than Status Points. I was saving them for when I reached the next level I needed to access more skills. My goal was to get the Dual Wield skill, which sounded like it would increase my attack speed and the damage I could inflict.

We soon reached Maliperum's room. Adina used the keys she stole from Maliperum to unlock the door, and we all went inside. The room on the other side was pretty nice. A large king-sized canopy bed with red drapes sat in the center, there were several massive pieces of furniture made from a type of rich-looking charcoal wood, tapestries hung from the walls, and the stone floor was covered by a soft rug. It was enough to make me forget we were in a dungeon.

"How decadent," Michelle said with a sneer.

"Maliperum was always vain," Adina agreed. "Anyway, if she has any potions or relics or something that will increase our level, they will be in that treasure chest."

Adina pointed to a treasure chest on the other side of the room. It was a lot more ornate than what Adina used to stash her items in, with gold inlays creating unique symbols and patterns along the surface. The wood was polished to a brilliant shine too. I'd say it went well with the rest of this opulence.

"Do you have the key to unlock it?" asked Michelle.

"It should be here," Adina said, jangling the keys. She walked up to the chest, but as she did, a strange feeling in my gut told me something dangerous would happen if she got too close. The hairs on my neck were raising. I wasn't one to ignore my feelings.

"Get back, Adina!" I shouted.

"What?"

Adina turned around as I rushed toward her. Just then, four legs and two arms extended from the chest, and it tried to grab her, but I wrapped my arms around her waist and yanked her back. She squealed as we landed on our respective backsides. However, she didn't say anything, because she too had seen that this chest was not quite what it seemed.

The chest had become a monster. It was an ugly looking thing. While it still maintained the basic appearance of a chest, it now looked like a creature with four spindly spider legs, two claw-like pincer arms, and a mouth with sharp, saw-like teeth.

"A mimic?!" Adina shouted in shock.

"So that's what that is?" I demanded. "How do we kill it?"

"The same way we kill any living creature," Michelle said as she created a sword of light in her hand. "Cut it into enough pieces, and it will die like everything else."

I wasn't really the kind of guy who approved of that kind of answer, but I knew she was right. Scrambling to my feet, I unsheathed my sword and charged toward the creature. I let my mana drain from me as I used Death by Piercing to damage the monster, but this mimic or whatever was stronger than it appeared. My sword glanced off its hard body despite using a skill.

"Its body is too tough!" Adina shouted. "Aim for its arms and legs!"

After leaping back to avoid its sharp pincers, Michelle and I charged forward again, dodging its arms before running underneath the monster. We swung as one, each of us cutting through a leg before running out the other side. The mimic screeched as it fell to the ground. That was when Adina raced forward and sliced one of its arms off with her nails.

As the mimic flailed around, I swung my sword into its remaining left leg, dis-legging the creature. No blood spurted out, but I guessed mimics didn't have blood since they were made of wood. Just like me, Michelle swung her sword and removed the last remaining leg before it could try and attack me. Then Adina finished it off by cutting its remaining arm off. The mimic screeched some more, but then its body shook before it once again transformed into a chest.

"Well... that wasn't too hard," Michelle admitted.

Adina smiled wryly. "Mimics are easy to kill once you know how... though they never actually die. This will revive again soon, so we need to check its contents and see if Maliperum has any treasure before that happens."

"Would you do the honors?" I asked with a chuckle.

"I'd love to."

With a skip and a bounce, Adina bent over to unlock the chest, giving me a perfect look at her amazing ass. I knew Michelle was glaring at me as I checked the succubus out. I ignored her. No matter what, I was still a man, and I had two sexy and strong women as traveling companions. I'd never do something like force them into a relationship with me, but I wasn't above admiring them every now and again, especially since one of them wore practically nothing.

"Heh. We hit the jackpot," Adina said, raising her body and shaking several vials filled with bright red liquid. The contents inside were bubbling. "Check these out."

"What are they?" I asked.

"Life Essence potions," Adina said while wearing her brightest smile.

CHAPTER 7

I ran down the hall, my feet slamming into the stone, causing the sound of my footsteps to echo all around me. Of course, that sound was drowned out by another sound. The sound of several dozen feet chasing after me and the loud croaking war cries being released by those creatures. I craned my neck to look behind me, grimacing when I saw two trolls and over a dozen imps hot on my tail.

"Why do I have to be the bait?"

It was a question I had asked myself several times. I still hadn't found the answer. Maybe it was just because I sucked at rock, paper, scissors. Even after doing this nearly twenty times, I still hadn't won a single time.

Lady Luck was a bitch to me.

Turning a sharp corner, I followed the path my party and I had laid out. There were no windows in this dungeon, which was built underneath the very crust of this planet, or dimension, or whatever this place was. All I saw were stone walls, a stone floor, stone ceiling, and the occasional stone column.

It didn't take more than five minutes before my target came in sight. A large door at the end of the hall I was in stood wide open. I raced through the door with barely sixty seconds to spare, then turned around, unsheathed my sword, and prepared for combat.

I wasn't even winded.

Even as a US Marine, running for several hours at a full-paced sprint would have at least left me winded and sweaty, but I no longer felt even mildly out of breath. I believed that was because of my current level. The last time I had checked my stats, they were much higher than what they'd been previously.

My current stats were:

Name: Bryan Jenson
Class: Magic Swordsman
Level: 57
Magic: Red/fire
Attack: 140
Agility: 130
Defense: 140
Magic Defense: 120
Mana: 100
Total Status Points available: 0

Special Skills:
Whirlwind Slash: Attack +5
Death by Piercing: Attack +5
Fire Slash: Attack +5
Fireball: Attack +5
Total Skill Points available: 12

Whether it was because of my level or some other reason, I was in a lot better shape now than I had been before.

On either side of the door stood Michelle and Adina. The two did not look any different now than they had been before. Michelle wore her toga-like robes and Adina was practically naked. However, Adina did have a few additional changes. Her tail was a little longer, and she now had horns that curved elegantly around her head. She gained those features after reaching level 30. I wasn't sure what level she was at now, but she said that she would gain wings after reaching level 50.

At that very moment, the imps and trolls raced in through the doorway, which Michelle and Adina slammed shut. The demons didn't seem to notice. Their eyes were focused solely on me.

I bared my teeth at them as I charged forward, moving my body into a Whirlwind Slash, which decimated the entire front force of imps, about half a dozen of them, and then I leapt back and unleashed a fireball that killed another two. The imps I had slain were cut in half, and their bodies fell to the floor before turning to dust. The imps I incinerated were burnt to cinders. The scent of burning flesh filled my nose, causing it to wrinkle.

Just then, Michelle and Adina threw themselves into the back flank, tearing apart the imps that were present.

Michelle's sword flashed out as she swung it. It buzzed and thrummed like a lightsaber. Because it was made from the light element, or the holy element, her attacks easily sliced through these creatures, which fell like wheat before a scythe. I heard that at her current level, one sword was all she could make, but after reaching level 60, she would be able to acquire a several new skills that allowed her to make more.

Meanwhile, Adina viciously tore into her opponents with her claw-like nails. Her attacks were nowhere near as elegant as Michelle's, who fought with a methodical style that was designed to minimize how much energy she spent. Wild and ferocious, she ripped flesh from bone and tore off limbs like a madwoman. If she started randomly cackling at some point, I wouldn't have been surprised.

Of course, for all the ferocity in her attacks, Adina wore a surprisingly stern face. Like Michelle. Neither of them seemed to take any joy in killing these demons. I was honestly glad for that. This task wasn't a pleasurable one, and someone who took pleasure in killing so much probably had issues I didn't want to deal with.

It wasn't long before only the trolls were left. Adina and Michelle each took one.

The one on the left tried to smash Adina into the stone floor, raising its big hands and slamming them on the ground like it was attempting to nail a hammer into wood. A loud rumbling echoed around us. The floor shook. However, his target had leapt into the air and was now descending toward him.

Adina reared her hand back and brought it down. The troll roared in anguish as her nails sliced through the flesh of its face like a hot knife through butter, blood splattering against the floor as it stumbled backward. With her teeth set in a thin line, Adina leapt forward, used its stomach to launch herself into the air, and spun around to launch a powerful kick that caught it underneath the chin.

She was a lot stronger than she looked, and that kick, which lifted the troll off its feet and made it crash onto its back, was the proof. The floor rumbled. I nearly fell on my ass, but I bent my knees and redistributed my balance to remain upright.

Once it was down, Adina landed on its chest. She raised her right hand, fingers extended to form a knife-shape, and brought the hand down. More blood sprayed from its body as she sliced into its throat. The troll spasmed several times but quickly died. Its body would take a little longer to disintegrate than the imps as Adina absorbed its Life Essence.

While Adina took care of her enemy, Michelle dealt with the one she had targeted. Unlike Adina, who still didn't have wings, Michelle flew through the air faster than a jet fighter. She flitted about like a hummingbird, which was a little shocking to see. The troll tried to swat her away. However, its attacks never came anywhere close to her. It always seemed to hit an afterimage or something similar.

Michelle darted in close and ran her sword along its stomach. Blood spilled from the wound. I nearly vomited when its intestines also tried to fall out, though the troll held a hand to its belly to keep them in—not that it mattered. Michelle darted back in, swung her sword, and removed its hands next. The hands fell to the ground. Then its guts spilled onto the floor, splattering with a sickening sound that churned my insides.

As the troll landed on its knees, a bloodcurdling scream escaping its throat, Michelle flew forward and swung one last time. The screaming abruptly stopped. Nothing seemed to happen at first, but then, ever so slowly, the troll's head fell off its body and rolled across the floor. Its body came not long after. It hit the floor with a loud rumble and went still.

I looked at the two as they both walked away from their kills and checked my stats. I ignored the one that told my level and looked at how much Life Essence I needed before I regained my next level.

Name: Bryan Jenson
Level: 57
Life Essence needed to reach next level: 1,259/1,500

I sighed. It looked like I still had a ways to go before I could reach the next level.

"Good work bringing those things here," Michelle said. "You've become very gifted at pulling in larger hordes of demons."

"Thanks, Chris!" Adina said with a cheerful yet beautiful smile. "It's only because of your hard work that I've managed to reach level 43 in such a short time!"

I wasn't sure how much time had passed in this place, but after using the Life Essence Potions to raise our levels, the three of us had begun grinding. We had one person find a group of enemies. Meanwhile, the other two would wait at a predetermined location, then ambush the horde chasing after the bait. Thus far, I was the only person who had played the bait.

"I'm happy I can help you two, really, but could someone else please be the bait next time?" I asked.

Michelle sighed, then nodded. "I suppose it is not fair to have you keep acting as the bait, so I will be the bait next time."

"Thank you," I said.

Adina waved her hand. "I'll be the bait after Michelle's turn. I think I'm at a high enough level now where I can do that and not get killed."

"Speaking of." I frowned. "How many more times should we do this today?"

"Let's do this… six more times," Michelle said after thinking about it for a moment. "I know we shouldn't rush this, but I really want to at least reach level 60. Once I've done that, I can use the skill Dance of a Thousand Swords. It will allow me to create multiple swords in the air and launch them at several enemies at once."

"I think level 60 is a good level to aim for," I admitted. At that level, I'd also unlock two new skills. The first was called Dual Wielding, which I guess would let me use two weapons at the same time. The second was called Shielder, which lets me wield a sword in one hand and a shield in the other.

"And I'll gain my wings once I reach level 60," Adina said, her eyes vibrant and glowing. "Once I get my wings, I can learn new skills too."

"What kind of skills do you learn at level 60?" I asked.

"I can learn Energy Blast," Adina said. "It's a skill that lets me fire energy balls from my hands. It can be linked with other skills as well. If I learn the Flight skill and Energy Blast, I can also learn Energy Bombardment, which lets me fire multiple energy balls at the ground, creating a series of massive explosions. It's a good skill for attacking small fries, though it's not as effective on a single powerful opponent—not unless my level is higher than theirs."

I gave her a nod to show I understood. On my other side, Michelle was thinking hard about something as we continued walking. I would have asked, but I figured she'd tell us whatever she was thinking about in due time.

Just as Michelle had said, she played the bait this time. We set up our ambush point, Michelle left, and then came back several minutes later with about twenty imps. There were no trolls, sadly, which earned more Life Essence points, but we still managed to raise our experience at least a little.

Adina played the bait next. She actually did a pretty good job. About three dozen imps, one troll, and a succubus chased after her. The battle was a lot more hard fought than before. I ended up engaged in combat with the succubus, who tried to use her allure on me. It felt a lot like my mind was wading through mud. Focusing on anything other than the woman's perky tits, bare pussy lips, and perfectly round ass was incredibly difficult.

From the smile on her face, she knew what she was doing to me.

"I really hope you don't think flashing your tits is enough to make me hard," I said to taunt the woman, who narrowed her eyes and hissed at me. "It's bitches like you that give succubi a bad name."

"Blasted mortal!" the woman finally broke her silence and spoke. "Do not think I will let this insult go unpunished!"

"Come and punish me if you think you're capable of it," I said with a shrug. I tried to hide my smile after angering her, but I was sure I hadn't succeeded.

The woman hissed some more as she attacked with hers claws and tail. I avoided her left swipe, used my sword to block a swipe from her right hand, and grunted as her strength pushed against me and caused sparks to fly. At least her allure was gone. It seemed succubi really didn't have any true magical abilities until they reached level 50. Now that I was thinking about it, even Maliperum didn't have any magic. The most they seemed to possess was this odd allure that made it easy to get distracted, but I had been living with Adina for quite some time now, so they didn't affect me very much.

One thing succubi did have, however, was incredible physical strength.

I grimaced as she slammed her nails into my sword. My arm was knocked wide, which opened me up to her attack. She tried to stab me through the chest with her right hand, but I leapt back to avoid it, then came back in with a thrust. Death by Piercing. As I felt the mana drain from my body, my sword seemed to glow as I stabbed at her.

She avoided my attack.

These succubi were an awfully limber race, able to contort their bodies in ways I'd never seen a human do before. She bent her torso at an angle that seemed to defy gravity. Consequently, this also caused her tits to move away from each other as if they were also being dragged down by gravity. My blade went right past her, not even grazing her body. In fact, my sword literally slid right through the valley of her breasts without drawing blood. She knocked my sword aside and came back up to attack me again, but I blocked her blow, even though it sent me skidding across the ground.

Since she could avoid attacks meant for an individual, I decided to use an attack meant for multiple opponents—Whirlwind Slash—which she also evaded. However, I noticed that my attack grazed her side. It drew blood, causing her to hiss and retreat as he held a hand to her torso. Her crimson eyes narrowed at me, but I grinned before launching a Fireball.

The cooldown time for Death by Piercing was over. As the succubus dodged my Fireball, I rushed in and used the attack again. Because she was too busy dodging the fireball, she was not able to dodge me again, and my sword sank into her chest. She looked down at the hilt of my sword, which I soon yanked out of her. The succubus fell to the ground with a thud. Her body didn't so much as twitch as she looked up at the ceiling, her eyes glazed over in death.

About thirty seconds after she died, her body burst into dust.

I learned from Adina and Michelle that demons turned into dust when they ran out of Life Essence. The person who killed them absorbed their Life Essence when they died, and then they disappeared. Adina had another talent called Essence Drain, which is how she absorbed Maliperum's Life Essence even though I killed her, but that was a rare skill specific to her. She called it a genetic skill. In either event, learning about this made me wonder what would happen if someone died without having their Life Essence absorbed. Would they remain here as a corpse and just rot?

Shaking my head, I checked my stats and saw that I had gained a level along with two more Skill Points and twenty more Status Points. I noticed after reaching level 55 that I gained two skill points instead of one. I wondered what that meant, but I honestly didn't have a clue, so I tried to put it out of my mind.

I saved the Skill Points and only allocated my Status Points.

Name: Bryan Jenson
Class: Magic Swordsman

Level: 58
Magic: Red/fire
Attack: 140
Agility: 140
Defense: 140
Magic Defense: 120
Mana: 110
Total Status Points available: 0

Special Skills:
Whirlwind Slash: Attack +5
Death by Piercing: Attack +5
Fire Slash: Attack +5
Fireball: Attack +5
Total Skill Points available: 14

After that, I checked my level stats and saw that I was at 25/2,000 before I reached my next level… which meant it would probably take a long time before I reached level 60. Whenever I reached a new level, it took more Life Essence before I could reach the next one. Back when I was level 50, it only took me 1,000 Life Essence to reach the next level.

We did draw in and ambush several more demon hordes. I didn't gain a level during that time, though I was now at 1,325/2,000 because I had fought several trolls and another succubus, which earned me more Life Essence points.

We eventually went back to Adina's hideout, which hadn't changed much… except for the new bed. Adina had thought it was a shame that Maliperum had such a nice bed and wasn't even going to use it anymore, so we'd pooled our strength together and moved the bed here. It had been a pain in the ass. However, we now had a better place to sleep than before.

A strange perfume pervaded the room now as well. It came from a series of incense that were burning along the room. The scent was soothing, a combination of lilac and lavender... I think. It was a very floral scent. These were also from Maliperum's room. There was nothing special about them. They were just incense.

"We should get some sleep," Michelle suggested. "We'll have to keep doing this tomorrow."

"Yeah, and I'm tired." Adina grabbed me by the hand and smiled as she dragged me toward the bed. "Come on, hug pillow. We're going to bed."

"At least let me remove my armor first," I muttered before undoing the catches for my chestplate, pauldron, gauntlets, and greaves. I also slipped out of my boots. Adina waited impatiently for me to finish, arms crossed as she tapped her foot against the ground. I wondered when she had removed her boots once I saw them sitting by the bed.

I didn't resist Adina's pull as she drew me onto the bed and pushed me down. I really had nothing to complain about, especially when Adina laid down at my side and nestled her body against mine. The feeling of her succulent breasts pushing into me, so soft and elastic I was reminded of two pillows, was like being trapped between heaven and hell. Since they were only covered by thin strips that kept her nipples from showing, I could feel practically all of her. Those feelings were only amplified when she hooked a leg around mine.

Michelle looked at us with a small scowl; it was easy to see she didn't approve of our intimacy, but I wasn't going to let that bother me. It wasn't like Adina and I had sex. Cuddling was about as far as we'd gone.

Of course, it could have been that Michelle was jealous. She had glanced my way on any number of occasions. However, I didn't know if I should bring that up or not. We were in a life threatening situation, where each new day could be our last, and I had no desire to add any kind of relationship drama to the party. At this junction, we needed to trust each other to watch our backs. That wouldn't happen if we were arguing over what our relationship was.

The archangel laid down on the bed next to us, but she turned around so she wasn't facing us. I sighed. It really was difficult knowing what I should do and say right now. However, I did my best to put that out of my mind for the moment and closed my eyes. Hopefully, I wouldn't have any dreams tonight.

***

I dreamed of fire, bullets, and blood.

I was surrounded by flames. They licked at my kevlar vest and pants as I ran through the war torn battlefield. Bodies lay strewn around me.

I wasn't alone. Comrades raced by my side, but they died one by one. Some received a bullet to the head. Others went up in flames when they stepped on a landmine. Even more went down under a hail of bullet fire, their kevlar vests unable to withstand the intense heat. Soon, it was just me and my best friend.

Yet soon, even my best friend went down, stepping in front of me when the enemy unleashed a hailstorm of bullets. I fell to the ground and looked up. Blood splattered against my face as his body shook back and forth. It felt like I could almost see the bullet wounds as they exited his body. My eyes widened and my heart grew cold and fearful as the bullet fire ceased and my friend's lifeless corpse fell to the side.

"No! No no no no NO!"

I screamed as I ran over to my friend's side and tried to rouse him. It didn't matter. As I turned his body over, rolling him onto his back, I found lifeless eyes gazing up at me.

"CHRIS!"

The scream erupted from my throat as I sat up, my breathing heavy, my eyes wide, and my body shaking. The scent of blood still filled my nose. It was almost enough to make me wretch. It took me a moment to realize I wasn't on the battlefield.

My scream woke the other two. Michelle leapt out of the bed, a sword of light appearing in her hand as she shifted into a battle stance. Meanwhile, Adina shrieked in shock, tried to stand up, became tangled in the bedsheets, and fell back onto the bed. She squirmed around for a moment, but realized she was getting more tangled the longer she struggled.

"Bryan?" Michelle realized there was no enemy, released the light sword, and looked at me with a concerned frown as she sat back down. "What is wrong? Why are you screaming?"

"N-nothing." I tried to smile, but I don't think it reached my eyes. "Just a bad dream."

"Do you want to talk about it?" asked Adina as she carefully untangled herself from the bedsheets.

"I..."

I was about to tell them not to worry, that it wasn't something they needed to think about, but I paused. In all the years since it happened, I had never once told anyone about what I had experienced. I never talked about what happened to me, what it felt like, or anything really. I'd bottled up my feelings and let them fester.

But it wasn't like I didn't want people to know. There had been times where I thought it would be nice to tell someone, but I never did because I was afraid they wouldn't understand. Maybe... maybe it was time I actually said something.

"I... used to be a soldier in my world's army—I was a member of the Special Forces for the United States Marines," I said. "This was a few years back. At the time, my best friend and I had joined because we had a member of the Marines give a speech at our school. We got into the Marines soon after graduating, went through training, and joined their Special Forces. We went on numerous missions for them, but…" I trailed off for a moment, shook my head, and smiled self-deprecatingly as I continued. "I don't think we had any idea about how hard the Special Forces were, of what they did and how dangerous it was."

"What happened?" asked Michelle, placing a hand over one of mine.

I hadn't realized I was clenching my hands until she did this. My hand slowly relaxed. Adina sidled up to my other side and leaned into me. I know it was probably weird to take comfort from a demon, but hers and Michelle's presence really helped settle my nerves.

"Well… to make a long story short, I saw a lot of death, enough that it now haunts my dreams." I released a soft sigh. "Even my best friend eventually died. It was actually on our last mission. We had been ordered to retrieve some data that had been stolen by a foreign government. We were able to sneak into the facility it was being kept, steal it, and get back to the extraction point, but… I don't know. It must have had a trace on it because the next thing I knew, we were being ambushed by enemy forces. My friend shielded me from an attack and died. After that, I quit the Marines. I've been having nightmares ever since."

While I wouldn't say I felt better letting this all out, I wouldn't lie and say I felt nothing either. It was a little relieving to get all that off my chest.

I looked at the two girls. Michelle's compassionate gaze was enough to soothe the soul of anyone who looked at it, and I was no different. However, it was Adina who surprised me, though I was beginning to realize being a succubus didn't change who she was on the inside, which was a warm and caring woman.

"I guess we aren't the only ones who have been through a lot," Adina said as she stroked my arm. Her soft hands felt incredible on my skin. It was enough to make me forget her nails could become extremely long and tear through flesh as easily as paper.

"The human world has always been one filled with death and mayhem. I've know this for a long time." Michelle paused as she squeezed my hand. "But I don't think I ever realized how it affected humans. I wish there was something I could do to make this all better, to take away your pain, but that's sadly impossible."

"It's fine." I smiled at Michelle and Adina. "I think just having people with me is enough. I've never shared this with anyone before. It's… nice."

Adina grinned as she leaned forward, until her lips were practically kissing my ear. "You can share anything with me. Just speak up whenever you need to talk."

"You can also feel free to share your hardships with me," Michelle said as she grabbed my arm and pulled me away from Adina. She glared at the succubus, who frowned at her, and then shifted her kind gaze back to me. "I would be more than willing to listen to you whenever you wish to get something off your chest. As your partner and an archangel, it is my duty to share your burdens."

"Well… we succubi are great listeners!" Adina grabbed my other arm and yanked me toward her. I was completely certain she just yanked my arm out of its socket.

"So are archangels!" Michelle added with a yank of her own, and it took everything I had not to groan in pain.

"If sharing my burdens is going to include having you two fight over me like this, maybe I shouldn't share anything with either of you," I shot back.

Adina and Michelle let go of me at the same time.

"M-my apologies, Chris," Michelle said, looking contrite. "I don't know what came over me."

"Me too. I'm sorry," Adina added with a soft frown. "I just don't want you two leaving me out of anything."

These two had good intentions, and I believed they were good people—well, a good angel and demon—but the way they sometimes bickered like this could be annoying, especially when they were fighting over me in some way, shape, or form. It wasn't cute at all.

At some point, I knew I would have to speak with them. I wanted to know what I was to them, but I couldn't say anything until I knew what they were to me. At the moment, my emotions were all jumbled together, and there was also the fact that I didn't know how long I would remain here. Even if I confessed now, there was a good chance we'd never see each other again after we killed Naamah. Was there any point in saying something if that was the outcome?

I sighed.

Relationships on their own were complicated.

Relationships inside of another dimension/world/whatever with one angel and one demon were even more complicated.

Fuck my life.

CHAPTER 8

While I did have some issues with the relationship between myself and the two beautiful women at my side that did not stop us from continuing our current path. Each day we scouted out good ambush points, and each day one of us would act as the bait and draw several demons into an ambush. Like this, the days passed, and our levels continued to slowly rise.

I was a little concerned about being discovered by Naamah, but Adina told me not to worry about that.

"She doesn't come down this far," Adina explained. "Because she is at heart just a puppet. She is under the control of the master of this fortress, the powerful ruler Asmodeus. He's one of the nine rulers of hell. Like us succubi, he is the epitome of lust, but he is so much stronger than we are. Even my mother was wary of him."

"I see. So the person who Brad and the others were after was this Asmodeus," I said with a sigh. "However, if they can't even defeat Naamah, there is no way they'll be able to beat Asmodeus."

"Probably not," Adina agreed.

It was currently another day of grinding to level up, and we'd just finished off another small army of imps. I noticed that we were running out of prey to kill. This also meant our levels weren't rising as quickly. Imps did not even have much Life Essence to begin with, especially when compared to the much more powerful troll.

"This isn't working anymore," Michelle said with a sigh. "I'm nearly at level 60, but the amount of Life Essence we gain from killing imps just isn't enough. What's more, with less and less enemies appearing, I fear there may not be enough in this area of the dungeon to give us that last boost we need."

"What is your level?" I asked Adina, who scrunched her nose cutely before answering me.

"It's only at level 40 right now," she admitted.

"And I'm still at level 58," I said before grimacing. "Let's try this a few more times. If nothing else, the grinding will help Adina catch up to us. If we can let her reach level 50, then maybe we can take a crack at Naamah despite not being at the level we want."

"I suppose you bring up a good point." Michelle glanced at Adina, who glanced back and smiled. While the archangel didn't smile, her lips did twitch as if she was resisting the urge. "We'll do that then. If nothing else, I would like all of us to be capable of defending ourselves should the need arise."

With our decision set, we kept to our current course, but we didn't bother setting ambushes anymore. We sought out monsters and killed them. Since Adina was the lowest level among us, we had her kill the vast majority and merely focused our efforts on keeping her from being overwhelmed. Adina quickly went from level 40 to level 41, then 42, 43, all the way to 49.

I also ended up gaining a single level. When that happened, I did what I always did and allocated status points to my stats.

Name: Bryan Jenson
Class: Magic Swordsman
Level: 59
Magic: Red/fire

Attack: 140
Agility: 140
Defense: 140
Magic Defense: 140
Mana: 110
Total Status Points available: 0

Special Skills:
Whirlwind Slash: Attack +5
Death by Piercing: Attack +5
Fire Slash: Attack +5
Fireball: Attack +5
Total Skill Points available: 16

For a little while, I wondered if maybe I should use some of my skill points, but I was wary about using them when I knew there were better skills to spend those points on. I kept telling myself I could spend them once I reached level 60. Of course, even though I told myself this, I also recognized that I had a slight hoarding habit. Back when I was younger and played RPGs, I would always hold onto my skill points and not use them… and then I'd often end up beating the game without having ever spent more than maybe half the skill points I earned.

"I don't think we're going to gain anything more from picking off small fry in this part of the dungeon," Michelle said after we had returned to Adina's secret hideout.

The three of us were sitting around on the large bed. I no longer wore the armor of a magic swordsman. My black shirt and pants stretched across my body. Meanwhile, Michelle had her legs crossed as she leaned against a set of pillows. Her toes wiggled several times as if they were thinking like their master. On my other side was Adina, who was sprawled regally on her side and caressing her hips in a manner that just begged me to touch her. I wasn't sure if she realized how sexy she was being, but that was neither here nor there.

"So you think we should confront Naamah?" I asked.

"I think we don't have a choice," Michelle admitted.

"I'm not so sure that's a good idea." Adina grimaced as she ran a hand down her inner thigh. My eyes were automatically drawn to her plump pussy lips, visible underneath the tight strip of fabric covering her crotch. "Do not forget how powerful she is right now. She has at least eleven whole levels over you, and me and Bryan aren't as strong yet."

"So what do you suggest?" asked Michelle. "We can't stay here. Nothing good will come of it."

"There is a way," Adina admitted.

"A way to do what?" I asked.

"A way for us to get stronger," she answered.

I shared a glance with Michelle, who looked as confused as I felt, and then looked back at Adina. She was watching us. She stared into our eyes, her own vibrantly glowing blue eyes filled with expectation.

"What way is that?" I asked.

"One way is to Soul Bind with this world," she said. "You can't do that because you're just an avatar, but me and Michelle can… though I'm not sure if Michelle will want to since the nature of this world is the exact opposite of hers."

"I cannot," Michelle admitted. "This world symbolizes death, decay, and all things negative. It would conflict with the holy power given to me from my world. I am already Soul Bound to the seven heavens, which has given me increasingly powerful abilities over light and life. Soul Binding with this world would have the negative effect of making me weaker than I am now."

I still wasn't clear on this Soul Binding they spoke of, but I understood the basics of it. By synchronizing themselves with a world, they would become Soul Bound with that world, which greatly increased their abilities in a particular type of magic. My only real issue was I didn't know how a person would go about doing this. I kept imagining some weird old hermit meditating inside of a cave to gain enlightenment.

"That will also take a long time," Michelle added. "Especially since you have not tried to Soul Bind a world yet."

"Yeah…" Adina scratched the back of her neck and gave Michelle a sheepish smile. "That's why I'm suggesting the second way."

"And that is?" I prompted.

"You two have sex with me," Adina said.

"… huh?"

I actually needed a moment to register her words and comprehend them. It felt like my mind had suddenly crapped out on me. Michelle was in an even worse state. She looked like someone had zapped her in the face with a taser.

"Now, before either of you flip out or anything, just hear me out." Adina raised her hands in a "calm down and listen" gesture. I continued to stare. Michelle crossed her arms. "You both know I'm a succubus, right? Well, we succubi are a race that lives for the soul purpose of seducing and having sex with men. Our torture method is to literally have so much sex with someone that we turn them into a drooling mess. However, sex isn't just something we do. A lot of our powers are derived from the act."

"That is absolutely disgusting," Michelle said.

Adina puffed out her cheeks. "Don't be rude. It's how we're made."

My thoughts raced several miles a minute as I stared at this creature, who was now sitting up and earnestly looking at me with those vivid eyes of hers. It was hard to resist. Truth be told, I wasn't sure I wanted to resist, but I still did if only so I could understand what was happening.

"So… you want me to have sex with you… in order to increase your powers?" I asked.

"Yes." Adina nodded, then paused. "Well, it's not just that. I mean, if you'll let me be honest for a moment here, I really just want to have sex. I've wanted to have sex with you for a while now, but I haven't done anything because me and Michelle agreed to wait until the situation settled down."

"You and Michelle were going to wait to do what?" I asked.

"Isn't that obvious?" Adina said as Michelle looked down at the bedsheets. I noticed her cheeks were red. "We were going to tell you that we love you."

"You love me?"

I stared blankly at these two for a moment, not quite comprehending, or maybe not wanting to comprehend, what they were saying. They loved me. The idea was not… unfathomable.

I had wondered every so often these past few days if one or both of them might have had feelings for me. Adina was very obviously affectionate. She hugged me in her sleep, hugged my arm when she was awake, and often got in my personal space. I could see her having feelings for me, though I think I chalked up most of personality to her just being a succubus. But Michelle? The woman was incredibly kind and always worried over me, but she was an angel, a being who was supposed to be perfect and not at all into sex and romance. While I knew she had emotions, I wasn't sure if she would feel love for a mortal.

"Was that not obvious?" asked Adina, leaning forward and crawling over until she was right in my face. Her warm breath washed over my lips, and the scent of vanilla hung in the air as she bore into me with those beautiful eyes that had no pupils. "I'm pretty sure I made it obvious that I have feelings for you."

"I guess you have," I admitted, then glanced at Michelle. "But…"

When she saw my eyes on her, Michelle turned her head and crossed her arms. Her wings flapped a little in agitation as a blush spread across her cheeks. The pale pink coloration created an image of pure and virginal beauty.

"It's not… like my feelings are all that strong," she admitted. "I don't even really understand it myself, but I… well, even I understand that the way my heart races when I look at you is more than simple camaraderie."

Adina nodded as if agreeing with Michelle's words and turned to me. "And what about you? Are you telling me you don't feel anything for us? Nothing at all?"

As Adina and Michelle gazed at me with expectation in their eyes, I thought about how I should answer. Did I have feelings for them? It had been so long since I felt emotions like love that I didn't really know.

After losing every person I'd ever partnered with in the military, including my best friend, I distanced myself from everyone. I stopped talking to my family and women became nothing but bed warmers. I had refused to ever let myself become close to anyone, because I knew better than most what kind of pain you'd suffer from when someone you loved was taken away. I didn't want to experience that again.

But I also knew I had to make a choice. Here. Now. I understood that the situation would not let me run from my feelings, which meant I had to confront how I felt about these two.

The answer was… surprisingly simple. I think it had been staring me in the face this whole time, and I had just refused to look at it.

"I do love you two," I admitted, frowning very slightly as I felt my heart quiver. I placed a hand against my chest as if to steady myself, then looked at them with more confidence. "I feel the same way you two do."

"Then there's no problem!" Adina clapped her hands together. "Since you feel the same way, let's get right down to having sex." She tilted her head and smiled at me and Michelle. "And we even have the perfect bed to do it on. Aren't you two glad we lugged this thing all the way back here now?"

While I was still uncertain, since I'd already said what I felt, there wasn't much sense in hesitating anymore. I looked at Michelle. However, she wasn't looking at me. In fact, she seemed to be looking at anything but me and Adina, as if she was purposefully avoiding our gazes.

"Is this really something you're okay with?" I asked.

"W-what do you mean?" Michelle stuttered.

"I mean... I'm a human and Adina is a demon." I gestured to myself, then Adina. "Is being with us not going against God's teachings... or something like that?"

"There are no teachings I know of that say we can't have a relationship with whomever we want." Michelle still wasn't looking at me as she shrugged. "What's more, I... I'm not sure it matters anymore. I don't even know what's happening up in Heaven. I don't know whether my people are safe, or if the rebellion is still going on... I have no idea. But I do know our forces were overwhelmed. Even if there were some precepts that state an angel cannot fall in love with a human, I'm not sure it matters anymore."

"I think I understand," I said slowly, frowning just a little.

Michelle hadn't given up on returning home, but she wasn't certain she even could return home. I felt for her. At the moment, I wasn't sure how to return to my original body. I couldn't log out, which meant I probably needed to find a portal, but there hadn't been a single portal in the entire dungeon so far.

While Michelle and I looked at each other, Adina pouted and got back on all fours. She crawled forward like a cat, or maybe even a panther, her large breasts hanging from her chest and swinging with hypnotic motions that drew my eyes toward them. The smile on her face became increasingly seductive as she put one hand in front of the other, invariably pushing her breasts together as she crawled over to me on all fours.

"Since everyone now understands where we all stand, I think holding back is pointless," she said with a breathless tone.

I would have asked what she meant by that, but I didn't need to. Adina reached me and suddenly lunged forward. A pair of indescribably soft lips hampered mine. Adina's mouth tasted like the finest ambrosia in the entire world. As she placed her hands on my shoulders, pushing me down so she could straddle me, her tongue penetrated my mouth and rubbed against my tongue.

It was electric.

My restraints broke as she kissed me. I kissed back, passionately, and maybe even a little desperately, my hands going to her backside and landing on her fine ass. Maybe it was because she was a succubus, but her ass was perfect. She had a perfectly heart-shaped ass that was both firm yet soft. As I grasped it between my hands, my fingers sinking into her skin, and Adina moaned into my mouth as she began grinding her pussy, still barely covered by cloth, against my leg.

As she ground her covered mount against me, blood rushed to my dick, causing it to swell and grow unbearably stiff. I suddenly realized these annoying pants were in the way, so I pushed Adina back and struggled to get them off.

"Let me help you," Adina said as she grabbed my pants and pulled them off me while I was still sitting down.

I realized somewhat belatedly that I wasn't wearing any kind of underwear when my dick sprang free and the cool, if somewhat stale, air caressed it. Was this because I was an avatar and avatars didn't wear underwear? No, no, no. I remember every character creation system from the RPGs I played as a kid. Characters always had underwear on, so why was I going commando?

Adina gazed at my cock, which was actually the same size as my real one. Damn. Whoever made this avatar body did a fine job. No wonder I felt so comfortable. As she gazed at my throbbing dick, Adina licked her lips and stared at it in fascination.

"So this is a penis," she muttered in wonder.

"Have you never seen one before?" I asked.

Adina shook her head. "No. Mother never let me join the others when they went to torture humans with pleasure. She said she had higher hopes for me and wished I could find happiness through other means. This is… my first time seeing one." Her cheeks flushed red as her eyes grew hooded. She gazed at me. "Can I touch it?"

"Feel free," I said.

With my permission, Adina reached out and grabbed my shaft. Her soft and somewhat cool hands felt so incredible on my hot cock that they caused it to twitch. Adina jerked her hands back when this happened, but then she touched me again and began slowly stroking the underside of my cock with her fingers.

"It's twitching," she muttered, a smile curving at her lips. "That's kind of cute."

I felt heat rise to my cheeks. I'd never heard someone call my dick cute before. It was honestly a little embarrassing and maybe even somewhat emasculating. Adina either didn't care or didn't realize this as she slowly leaned down and stuck out her tongue.

"Hrg!"

A soft groan escaped my mouth as the tip of Adina's tongue touched the underside of my cock. She moved, leaving a glistening trail of saliva as her tongue ran from the base of my dick all the way to my head. After giving me a thorough lick like I was a lollipop, she leaned back and blinked several times.

"Do you eat a lot of fruit?" she asked suddenly.

"Excuse me?" I asked, breathing just a little heavy.

"Strawberries. Do you eat them a lot?"

"Um… I sometimes have them for breakfast."

"Hmm… you taste kind of like strawberries."

I tasted like… a fruit? I wasn't sure how I felt about that, nor was I certain how I could taste like a fruit at all. I knew your diet could affect how cum tasted, but your dick? That was a new one.

Adina leaned back down, taking my dick in hand before she began licking it all over. Her inexperienced tongue covered me with her saliva. Even though it was clear she'd never done this before, her enthusiasm while licking my dick was so great that it sent electric jolts straight through my spine and into my brain. There was just something erotic about an inexperienced succubus tonguing my dick.

However, I didn't want to be the only one experiencing pleasure.

"Adina," I gasped, "bring that cute ass of yours over here please."

I wasn't sure Adina heard me at first, but then she moved around and swung a leg over my chest. With her legs now on either side of my chest, her ass and pussy were right in my face, still barely covered. In fact, her ass wasn't really covered at all. The thong-like garment was wedged between her asscrack. I wondered how to get it off at first, but then I found some hooks on either side of her hips and quickly undid them.

After peeling away the thong, I was finally able to gaze at her fully exposed pussy. She had no hair. I had expected that since I couldn't see any sticking out of that thong. A small hood rested at the very front of her pussy lips, hiding the clitoris. Unlike a lot of women I'd slept with, her pussy was a perfectly smooth line that looked like a pair of lips. She'd obviously never had sex. A virgin succubus. That was a new one. Her pussy traveled all the way up to her exposed asscrack.

I traced her pussy lips with my finger, then slowly pushed my finger passed her lips and caressed her labia minora. After simply letting my fascination wander, I grabbed her thighs, leaned up, and began licking her pussy. I ran my tongue from across her vagina from the top all the way to where it ended near her ass.

"Oh... that's... good," Adina moaned before she went back to licking my dick. "Mo peash!"

Since she seemed to enjoy my ministrations, I decided to go a bit further. As I pushed my tongue past her folds, I reached out toward her hood, worked out her clit, and began rubbing it. I applied a light pleasure to my strokes, listening to Adina as she moaned around my cock, which she had finally taken into her cute little mouth. The vibrations sent arcs of pleasure through my body, but I didn't want to cum first. I increased the pace of my rubbing and put more pressure on her clit, which pulsed several times. Adina's butt clenched for a second before her pussy began squirting her love nectar around my mouth.

Adina had a rich taste. I couldn't really describe it, but she was delicious nonetheless. I found that I couldn't get enough of her. As she released a flood of pussy juice, I lapped it all up, licking her pussy lips, thighs, and anywhere else to avoid missing a single drop.

While I was enjoying Adina's taste, Michelle was biting her lip, and I realized with some shock that she had spread her legs apart and was massaging her clit. She, unlike me, had been wearing underwear. However, her beautiful white panties were now hanging off one of her legs as she masturbated in front of us. It was so surprisingly lewd of her that I could hardly think for a moment. In that time, Adina began fondling my balls as she swirled her tongue around the head of my cock, which caused a powerful pressure to build up inside of me before it was released.

Adina must not have been expecting me to release such a huge flood of cum. She jerked back and coughed several times as she sat on my chest, cum dripping from her mouth.

"I'm sorry," I said. "I should have warned you that would happen."

I actually hadn't know that would happen. Even though I had accepted that I was not in some kind of virtual reality or whatever, I still didn't fully understand everything.

"It's fine." Adina closed her mouth and swallowed what was inside. "You definitely taste like strawberries."

"I'm not sure that's a good thing."

"It is a good thing," Adina assured. "I love strawberries."

Saying this, she scooped up what fell onto her breasts with her fingers. Now coated in white and sticky fluids, Adina stared at her fingers with fascination before she stuck them into her mouth. Her eyes were glowing as she licked my cum off her fingers. The act caused my flaccid dick to once again stiffen.

"It looks like you're ready for more." Adina turned around so she was facing me, then slid down my stomach until her ass rested against my cock. She rubbed that delicious backside against me, a smile growing on her face. "Are you ready for the next step?"

I glanced at Michelle, who was no longer stroking her pussy. She was resting against the head of the bed, her eyes glassy, hand hanging over her vagina, just barely concealing it from view. From her heavy breathing and the sweat covering her body, I could tell she had orgasmed.

I looked back at Adina.

"More than ready," I said, placing my hands on her hips.

Adina raised her hips. I helped her line her pussy up to my dick, and then she slowly went down. Inch after inch of my cock disappeared as her pussy lips slowly spread apart to accommodate me. Adina bit her lip with her sharp canines as an expression of pain appeared on her face. It seemed even virgin succubi experienced pain their first time. However, she didn't seem to have a hymen either. Her ass was soon resting on my thighs and balls and my dick was completely engulfed in her.

I breathed deeply as I tried to keep myself from blowing my load early. Adina's pussy was quite possibly the best I'd ever experienced. Her walls conformed to my dick, not too loose or too tight. It was like someone had created a mold of my cock and used it when making Adina.

As I wondered if this was another succubus power, Adina placed her hands on my chest, raised her hips, and brought them back down. The loud smack of her delicious ass hitting my thighs caused my thoughts to disappear as I focused on this gorgeous creature riding me. I kept a firm grip on her hips as I thrust upward, meeting her downward motion somewhere in the middle. Adina's soft moans became louder and louder as she increased her pace.

With her increased pace came an increased movement with her tits. They bounced up and down, up and down, constantly jerking and jiggling. The straps keeping her nipples hidden came undone. I could see her areolas and soft pink nipples. They were inverted. Now that was a surprise.

I sat up as Adina continued to ride me and sucked one of her nipples into my mouth. Adina screamed as she hugged my head to her chest. Meanwhile, I stuck my tongue inside of those inverted treasure troves, flicking it inside of her as I coaxed her nipple out. It stiffened as it emerged, and I didn't hesitate to swirl my tongue around it.

The heady scent of sex had completely overtaken the incense. Mine and Adina's bodies had become covered in a thick layer of sweat. We rubbed against each other as she bounced on my dick. I kept my mouth firmly attached to her nipple as my hands slid from her hips to her ass, which I smacked once before massaging it.

Adina's pussy tightened around me like it was trying to milk my body of all its essence, and then I came immediately after. As my seed flooded her womb, more of Adina's pussy juice flowed around me.

Her body went limp. I blinked in surprise as the woman's muscles and limbs became slack.

"Adina?"

When I received no response, I set the woman on her back and studied her. Adina's eyes were open, but they were glassed over like no one was home. She was breathing, which was good, and I watched as her chest rose and fell, causing her wonderful tits to jiggle. I wanted to play with them some more, but there was another person who we had been neglecting.

I turned to Michelle.

Michelle had begun rubbing herself again after me and Adina started having sex, but now she had stuck her toga into her mouth, muffling the moans that threatened to escape. This had also caused her toga to lift up. Before, it was hard to see what was happening because the toga kept shifting around, but now I could clearly see her furiously rubbing her clit. Her hand and thighs were drenched in juices, and a large stain was spreading out from underneath her bottom.

I went over to her.

"Let me," I said before grabbing her hips and pulling her toward me.

"Ah. W-wait!" Michelle released the toga in her mouth and suddenly shouted at me.

"Yes?" I asked.

"Um, uh... please be gentle," Michelle muttered. "I've... never done anything like this before."

I smiled. "I will."

As I laid her down, I positioned myself between her legs and began licking her thighs and pussy of all the juice she had already released. Her taste was lighter than Adina's. Not as thick. However, there was something refreshing about her that I couldn't grasp. As I cleaned her off with my tongue, Michelle released several soft moans that had a hint of shyness to them. It was so different from the enthusiastic Adina that I couldn't help but find it adorable.

It also made me want to hear what she sounded like when she was crying out in ecstasy.

"OOH!!"

Michelle released a loud scream and her hips jerked as I placed my mouth over her clit and flicked it with my tongue. At the same time, I pressed one of my fingers against her lips and slowly pushed my way inside. Her pussy walls pulsed as I curled my finger and searched for that sweet spot. I found it when her entire body convulsed, then rubbed it.

The scent of Michelle's sweat filled my nose, arousing me to continue what I was doing. Michelle's body shook, her thighs trembled, and her moans cascaded around my ears like a beautiful symphony. I wanted to hear more. When I looked up, I couldn't see her face, but I saw the way she was fondling her own tits, still covered by her toga. I wished I could see them in all their uncovered glory. Maybe later. For now, my goal was to make her orgasm.

Michelle's back arced as she came. I wasn't sure if this was the second time or the first, but her juices flowed around my fingers, which I removed as she slumped back onto the bed. I brought my hand to my mouth and sucked my fingers clean, enjoying her taste, then positioned myself between her legs and leaned over.

"Michelle?" I said. She blinked and looked at me. "Can I fuck you?"

"You can't," Michelle said immediately, turning her head. "You can't fuck me... but you can make love to me."

I gave her a helpless smile as I turned her head and leaned down for a kiss. I wasn't sure I recognized the distinction between fucking and making love, but I could tell this was important to her. My kiss was gentle and tender. Well, I hoped it was gentle and tender. At the very least, Michelle responded to me with an eager moan as she wrapped her arms around my neck and pulled me in.

As I kissed her, I grabbed ahold of my dick and pressed it against her sodden entrance. Unlike Adina, Michelle had a small patch of trim pubic hair, which I felt as I ran my cock over her. Her hair was very fine. I slowly pushed my way inside, a nasally gasp escaping my mouth as I realized she was much tighter than Adina. Once my cock was buried inside of her, I tried to pull out and found that moving was hard. It was like her pussy wanted to suck me in and keep me there.

"You're... you're inside," Michelle muttered with a breathless, shocked tone.

"I am," I said. "You're really tight."

"S-sorry."

"Why are you apologizing?" I chuckled as I leaned forward and kissed her nose. "I love how deliciously tight your cute pussy is."

"D-don't call it that. That's so crass." Michelle turned her head to once more look at something that wasn't me.

Another chuckle escaped my lips as I leaned down and placed my mouth against her neck. Michelle stiffened as a low moan escaped her lips. I began kissing my way along her neck, listening to the rise and fall in Michelle's pitch. It wasn't long before I found a small area on her neck that caused the greatest reaction. With a slight grin, I lightly bit down on her skin and sucked on it.

"Ooooh! W-what is this?!" Michelle sounded confused as her pussy convulsed around me, but I couldn't answer her question.

I rocked my hips and slowly began working my way out, pulling my dick out until a cool breeze hit the half that I managed to pull outside, then pushing back inside. Michelle moaned as she turned her head to kiss me. Her hands moved to my back, grasping at my shirt, while her legs wrapped around my hips. I felt a pair of feet lock on the small of my back. With every slow thrust inside of her, Michelle would help pull me in with her legs and feet, allowing me to reach so deep I felt like my dick was pressing against her cervix.

As our slow lovemaking reached a crescendo, I felt my balls and stomach tighten. With a muffled grunt, I released my seed deep inside of her. Michelle moaned into my mouth again. Her fingers gripped my shirt tightly and her legs shook as if the muscles were spasming. A moment passed before she relaxed, legs unhooking and falling to the bed, arms releasing me.

I slid out of her pussy with a wet plop and noticed I had creampied her. My sperm spilled from her pussy and onto the bed. I groaned when my dick tried to get hard again, but I was pretty spent. Rolling onto my side, I released several deep breaths and tried to slow down my heart rate.

As I laid there, Michelle turned over and snuggled into my armpit. I wrapped my arm around her shoulder in an almost unconscious gesture. Her warm body against mine was pleasant. I looked down at her and noticed that her wings had folded up against her back. Soft feathers brushed against my arm, tickling my knee.

I looked from her to Adina, who still seemed to be off in never never land. She was near the foot of the bed. A frown appeared on my face as I thought about picking her up and bringing her over into this small cuddle session, but I was so tired my eyes were already closing.

Sleep overcame me before I could think of doing anything else.

***

I woke up the next morning feeling oddly refreshed. Sitting up in bed, I noticed that neither Michelle or Adina were with me. That made me frown. However, just as I was about to grow concerned, a voice spoke up from my left.

"I see you're finally awake."

Glancing in the direction of the voice, I found Adina and Michelle, fully dressed and standing by the bed. Adina was all smiles while Michelle wore a small frown. The archangel placed her hands on her hips as she looked at me like a stern teacher who was about to lecture her student on his poor behavior.

"Come on. We need to get moving. We're going to confront Naamah."

I climbed off the bed and stretched my body out for a moment. I wasn't wearing any pants, so my dick was flopping around. Adina licked her lips like she was looking at a piece of prime beef, but Michelle blushed and averted her eyes. That was cute. As I put on my pants, I glanced at Adina, who had the most vibrant glow I'd ever seen. Michelle was glowing too, but the succubus's glow was actually physical, like there was a sheen of light overlaying her body. What's more, two new appendages were jutting from Adina's back.

Her wings.

They weren't very large and protruded from the middle of her back instead of her shoulder blades like I would have expected. They appeared almost leathery and reminded me vaguely of batwings, but I think that was because of the bone structure. As I stared at them, her wings flapped a little, and I looked from them to Adina's smiling face.

"You've reached level 50," I said with a small grin.

Adina giggled. "That's right." She thrust out her chest. "Thanks to you, I am now at level 52."

I nodded as I did the attached the belt with my sheath to my pants and began putting on my armor. If Adina was at level 52, then it meant we were ready.

It was time to face off against Naamah.

CHAPTER 9

Naamah was seated on her throne just like she had been the last time I came here. Back then I had been with Brad, Elric, and Vyra, but this time I was with Adina and Michelle—a succubus and archangel respectively, and also my… lovers? I don't think we had really defined our relationship, but yeah, I guess that was a good enough term to describe what we were to each other for now.

Our opponent had the same dark blue skin I remembered, sat with one leg crossed over the other, and was leaning back with the same look of arrogance from before. A smile curved her lips as we approached. I glanced at the strange yellow lines, which supposedly came from one of the worlds she was Soul Bound with.

According to Michelle, Yellow represented the power to boost morale and cast illusions. Meanwhile, her dark blue skin, which I believed was a mixture of black and blue instead of just pure blue, was the representation of water and death. It was very likely she could use spirits, sleep magic, create psychic shields, absorb negative energy, and control darkness. While I was confident we could take her, I wasn't gonna lie and say this wouldn't be a hard fight.

"I thought it was odd that Maliperum hadn't contacted me in so long," Naamah said, eyes narrowing. "The last time she talked to me, it was to inform me that you, human, were being incredibly difficult and resisting her interrogation methods. She said she had everything under control... but I guess that was a lie." She paused as her eyes shifted to Adina, who glared at her with a look of such viciousness it was honestly shocking. "Little Adina, are you really going to betray me after everything I have done for you?"

"You haven't done anything for me!" Adina shouted harshly. The anger in her voice was palpable.

"Oh, but I did." Naamah seemed to find Adina's anger amusing, for the smile on her lips grew wider. "I took you in when you had nowhere else to go. You have a place to call home because of me."

"You're the one who took my mother away from me!" Adina snapped. "Home? Ha! You stole my home from me, and then you enslaved me! It's because of you that I don't have a home!"

"Oh, my. How could you say something so cruel? This hurts me too, you know." Naamah raised a hand to her cheek in shock, as if she was appalled Adina would think her so cruel. It was clear to me that she was mocking Adina. "I had no desire to seal your mother away, but I simply had no choice. Your mother had gone insane and become a threat to the succubus race. I had to seal her for all our sakes."

This woman's words were like a sweet poison, spoken with a lilting voice that could bewitch the mind and make even the most stoic of warriors fall to her whims. However, mixed with those honeyed words was a biting venom. Even I could sense the ill-intentions pouring from this woman.

Michelle stepped forward before Adina could shout some more. A ball of light agglomerated in her hand, then extended and became a sword when she closed her fist around it. She pointed the sword at Naamah, eyes narrowed, mouth drawn into a stern frown.

"I do not particularly care about the squabbles between succubi," she said in a cold voice that could have frozen over Hell. "After I was blasted out of Heaven, you captured me, bound me to that wretched woman, and forced me to endure more humiliation than I care to remember. For that alone, I will kill you."

"Oh, dear. It seems I am really hated here. Well, I am fairly used to this. To become the Queen of all Succubi, one must be prepared for those who would despise her to rise up in rebellion. Very well. Allow me to show you the might I have acquired since becoming the ruler of this world."

Naamah stood to her feet, the action so smooth and sensual I felt a slight twitch in my mental state. She looked at us with those glowing red eyes as her wings extended from her back. Unlike Adina's, these were large and imposing, creating a uniquely intimidating aura that enhanced the sensual allure of her barely clothed figure. Her spaded tail swayed back and forth as the horns on her head glowed with a mysterious yellow light. The symbols running along her body became brighter.

My breathing caught in my throat, and then I suddenly felt a strange tug at my chest. The world around me shifted, turning gray, then fading out to create a small tunnel that led to Naamah, who stared at me with those beautiful and glorious eyes. As I stared at her, unable to see anything else, she extended a hand.

"Come to me," she said, her voice a seductive whisper. Oddly enough, her lips did not move. It was like she was speaking directly into my mind. "Come to me, and I shall grant you pleasure beyond imagining. Come to me, and I shall give you everything you could ever wish for."

I knew her words were like a poison, but even though I knew this, my heart lurched. It felt like something was yanking on me.

My mind was being overridden with something, a compulsion that told me to take her hand, that said everything would be better if I joined hands with her. I did my best to resist, but I could feel my willpower slipping.

I took a step forward.

Then a hand appeared in my left hand. It was small, soft, and delicate. I was so startled by the sudden sensation that the feelings around me slowly vanished, though the grogginess in my head didn't dissipate. However, when a second hand grabbed my other hand, I was able to fully dispel the feeling of fog clouding my head.

The world around me brightened, the darkness faded, and color returned as I glanced at my left and right sides. Adina and Michelle were holding my hands. It looked like they had sensed my inner struggle and decided to help me. I squeezed their hands back and glared at Naamah, who now wore a tiny frown.

"I see you two have already slept with him. This is... a most surprising turn of events," Naamah muttered. "Adina I can imagine, but you? Are you not the legendary Archangel Michelle who has been spoken of in prophecy? You are the one who was supposed to lead God's armies against us demons, right? And yet here you are cavorting with a demon. Most curious."

Michelle's glare didn't lessen as she continued drilling a hole into Naamah with her eyes. If looks could kill, I was certain this blue-skinned succubus would have been dead a thousand times over already.

"You are right. It was my job to lead Heaven's armies into battle against the demons, but the prophecy and my duty no longer matter. You know this as well as I do. The worlds have changed. Angels have free will, demons are disrupting the order of our worlds... even the other pantheons have risen up. The Greek gods are at war with their Roman counterparts. The Valkyries and Norse gods are struggling to prevent Ragnarok... ever since the change, our duty, our destiny, has been irrevocably erased. You and I are living proof of that. You would have never gone against Lilith and joined Asmodeus if this was not so."

There was a lot in her words that shocked me. It sounded like it wasn't just Heaven and Hell that were experiencing this change, but I knew I didn't have time to learn more. Right here, right now, I needed to focus solely on defeating the wretched creature before me.

"I suppose you are right," Naamah agreed with a slight smile. "Well, I guess that is enough talk. You have killed most of my henchmen, so it looks like I'll be battling against you myself. Though…" She giggled. "I don't expect this to be a very difficult fight."

As she spoke, Naamah's body wavered and disappeared. I gaped. However, before I could ask what the hell happened, the world around me changed. The dungeon walls disappeared to reveal a crimson sky, cracks spread across the ground, and fire erupted from these cracks like volcanic eruptions.

I was about to panic, but then I noticed something odd—a complete lack of heat. I couldn't feel any heat on my skin. My arms were not getting singed. It was as if I was staring at a 3D hologram.

Or an illusion.

"Do not think such a simple illusion will fool me!" Michelle shouted as she impaled the ground with her sword. Light erupted from the blade and spread across the ground like a ripple in the lake of a pond.

The illusion vanished.

"That is quite the power you have there." Naamah's voice echoed all around us. She hadn't appeared after the illusion dispersed. "I can see that you truly are the Archangel Michelle, general of God's armies. However, you have no hope of defeating me. You are completely outclassed."

As the woman spoke, several bolts of vibrant blew energy flew toward us from the left. I thought they were lightning bolts at first. However, when I cut into them using Fire Slash and steam rose around me, I realized they were water projectiles moving at incredible speed. I was fortunate. While fast, they did not move so quickly that I could not deal with them.

"Very impressive," Naamah said as I cut through her projectiles. "Now, let us see how you contend with this."

As she spoke, six glowing blue balls appeared around us, and Adina, Michelle, and I moved until we were back to back. I eyed the strange balls, which soon transformed into animal-like shapes. They looked like avians of some kind. Skeletal avians. They reminded me of the time I went to the Museum of Natural History and saw a skeleton of a Pterodactyl. However, these were blue, and had glowing red eyes embedded in their sockets.

"These are water spirits that she has infused with Red magic," Adina said. "It's one of her specialties. She summons a water spirit, mixes Red magic to strengthen them and increase their bloodlust, then lets them loose."

"How powerful are they?" I asked.

"I don't know, but they are definitely more powerful than the trolls we have been fighting," Adina admitted.

"It looks like we're about to find out how powerful they are," Michelle warned us. "They are coming."

The pterodactyl-like spirits darted forward with a flap of their wings, moving faster than I expected them to. One came up to me, and I slashed at it with my sword, but it performed a surprisingly deft barrel roll and avoided my swing. My blade struck the ground. Sparks flew over the surface. I gritted my teeth and leapt aside as another pterodactyl tried slamming into me from behind. It flew past the spot I'd been standing with a *woosh* of air.

Adina and Michelle were also doing their best to fight off these strangely nimble creatures.

Michelle shuffled across the ground and swung her light sword at the creatures who continued flitting about like hummingbirds, dodging her graceful attacks. Her eyes narrowed as a powerful energy spread across her body. I felt the hairs on my arms prickle as a bright golden energy erupted from her sword, which she swung out in a wide arc, causing a powerful wave shaped like a crescent to shoot forward. This wave slammed into one of the pterodactyls. It was engulfed by the golden light and faded from existence.

The other managed to escape destruction, but Michelle was already swinging her blade at it. A downward stroke sliced the monster in half.

While nowhere near as graceful as the archangel, Adina moved along the ground with incredibly nimble leaps. Her body was covered in a light pink glow. Her vibrant eyes were also glowing as she stared at the nearest pterodactyl, which slowed down as if her aura was calming it and drawing it in. That was a mistake. Seconds after it slowed, Adina created a ball of pinkish white energy in her palm and thrust her hand forward. The energy ball slammed into the spirit and caused it to explode.

The other spirit tried to attack her, but Adina was a lot stronger than she looked. She raised her hands, crossed her arms in a guard, and took its attack without budging an inch. While the spirit tried punching a hole into her by spinning like a drill and attacking her crossed arms, Adina swung her arms out and knocked it back. The spirit spun out of control. By the time it regained its balance, Adina had already risen her left leg high into the air and smashed it down on the creature in a powerful heel drop. The ground cracked underneath her heel and the spirit burst apart from the pure physical force of her attack.

While those two were dealing with their pterodactyl spirit... whatevers, I was fighting off my own two spirits. They darted around me, making hard to hit targets. I soon grew frustrated with my inability to cut them. With a low growl escaping my throat, I bent my knees, held out my sword, and spun around. Mana was pulled from my body as my blade began glowing. A powerful wave of energy blasted from my sword extending in all directions.

Whirlwind Slash.

The area attack was one that could only be dodged if the person I was attacking moved out of its range, but while these creatures were fast, I don't think they expected such a powerful attack. The energy caught them in the chest and sliced through them. Their bodies were cut in half. As they fell to the ground, their bodies dispersed into particles of light.

Clapping echoed around us.

"Bravo. Very good. You three are quite troublesome." Once again, Naamah's voice seemed to come from everywhere and nowhere. "However, do not be too pleased with yourself. That was only the opening act. I merely needed time to unleash my true attack."

A loud rumbling shook the floor around us, and I grimaced as something large and imposing walked down the stairs and came to stand in front of the empty throne. It was that creature from before. Like last time, it fiercely gripped a pair of claymores in its hands as it glared at us with glowing red eyes hidden behind its demonic helmet.

"This doesn't look good," Michelle murmured.

"Great." Adina grimaced. "It's her guardian beast."

"What's that?" I asked.

"A creature she can summon thanks to her Soul Binding," Adina answered. "I don't know how powerful it is, but it's definitely stronger than everything else we fought so far."

"Well… that's just great," I said before the massive creature lurched forward. The ground beneath its feet cracked as it shot at us with an astonishing amount of speed. It was so fast we almost couldn't get out of the way in time.

As I raced to the left, Adina raced toward the right and Michelle shot over its head. The creature stopped on a dime. It spun around and attacked me, swinging its massive claymores with powerful arcs that cut the air.

I knew better than to let those things hit me. I leapt backward and avoided its powerful swings, though it still managed to push me back from the sheer force. While I was trapped in its sight, Adina raced forward from behind and slammed a powerful kick into the creature's knees. It went down onto a single knee.

"Now, Michelle!" Adina shouted as she leapt back.

Michelle was flying above the creature, her wings flapping as she created several swords of light, which hovered around her body. With a wave of her hand, those swords flew into the creature. I wasn't sure what I was expecting. However, most of the swords bounced off it with a clash of sparks and a metallic clanging sound. Only one managed to pierce through its armor. It slid into the junction between its chestplate and helmet, one of the few parts that weren't protected.

The creature released a muffled roar that sounded like anger as it stood on its feet and tried to attack Michelle, who flitted out of the way. With its back now turned to me, I raced toward it, mana draining from my reserves as I stabbed my blade forward and unleashed Death by Piercing. My sword sank into its left knee. Blood spurted from the wound as it fell down with another loud roar.

Sensing an opportunity, Adina raced over and jumped into the air. A glowing ball of energy appeared around her hand. As she fell forward, she slammed that energy ball into the knight's helmeted face. A massive explosion went off and rent the air. The creature fell onto its back with a loud rumble that shook the ground, and I didn't hesitate to use this opportunity. I leapt onto its chest, held the sword in a two-handed reverse grip, and stabbed it down.

The monster struggled for a moment as my blade penetrated its head, but it quickly stopped and went limp. After another moment, the monster burst into ash, and I landed back on the ground. Adina and Michelle came back to my side.

"Tch!" Naamah clicked her tongue. "You three really are a lot of trouble... but no matter. I have plenty more tricks up my sleeve."

"Adina?" I said as I held my sword at the ready and looked around.

"Naamah is a powerful illusionist and user of Blue magic, though she can also use Red and Black magic," Adina explained as if she knew what I wanted to know. "Her preferred method of fighting is summoning spirits and infusing them with power to fight for her. Meanwhile, she will hide behind an illusion and simply wait for us to die."

"So in order to defeat her, we need to dispel the illusion she is hiding behind," Michelle said with a nod. "I have a spell that can dispel illusions, but it requires time to activate. Can you two keep me safe while I gather the necessary mana to cast it?"

"You can count on us," I said as I readied my sword.

"Hmph." A snort echoed around the room. "I do not know what you have planned, but it won't work! Come, Water Serpent!"

Water molecules gathered before us, swirling around as they coagulated several feet from our position. As they gathered, they took the shape of a giant snake at least ten yards long, with glowing red eyes, and an undulating body that was partially translucent. It hissed at us as its body changed from watery blue to deathly black. It looked like it was being encased in scales of darkness. As the creature was fully formed, it slammed its tail against the ground,

Swordsman of the Rift   140 cracking the stone floor and causing a loud rumbling sound to echo around us.

"What is this?" I asked in shock.

"It's just another spirit she summoned," Adina said. "However, this one is a lot more powerful than those sprites. It might even be as powerful as that bone knight. She's infused Black magic into it. You need to be careful. This kind of magic allows it to absorb negative emotions. The more negative your thinking is, the more powerful it becomes."

"So we need to battle it with positive thoughts?" I chuckled. "How clichéd."

"Excuse me?" Adina looked confused.

"Nothing. Anyway, let's take this thing down."

"Right!"

While Michelle stood back, Adina and I raced toward the giant serpent, which narrowed its eyes at us before opening its mouth. It spat several globules at us. Adina and I split apart to dodge the attacks. I glanced at one of the spheres as it struck the ground, which immediately began hissing as it melted through the floor. So this thing could also spit out a highly acidic venom? Good to know.

I reached the creature first. Fire appeared along my sword as I used Fire Slash, slicing into the monster with everything I had. It didn't do much. I felt some resistance as I cut through the serpent's body, but there was no blood nor did the creature hiss in pain. Well, I guess if it was just a summoned spirit, then maybe it couldn't feel pain.

While my attack didn't appear to do any real damage, it did seem to recognize me as a threat. It lifted its tail and slammed it toward me. I leapt away as the tail smacked into the ground, once more creating cracks that spread along the surface. Before it could retract its tail, I let out a roar and sliced my sword down, hacking into the tail, which separated from the rest of its body.

The creature hissed at me, but that was all it could do as Adina leapt into the air, spun around, and descended toward its head. She reared her fist back and brought it down. Her attack had so much power behind it that a shockwave spread out from where she'd struck the snake and several of its scales cracked. Adina then used the kinetic energy from her punch to push herself off the snake. She flipped through the air, flapped her wings, and landed on her feet several yards away.

Hissing at Adina, the serpent spat several balls of acidic venom. Adina used her powerful leg muscles to push herself off the ground and break into a sprint. She flapped her wings and soon gained lift, though she stayed low to the ground as she swerved left and right. Her speed was impressive, allowing her to keep ahead of the creature's attacks. While she was dodging the acid, I rushed up behind the beast and leapt onto its scaly back. Mana drained from my body as my sword began glowing. With a vicious thrust, I plunged the sword into the back of the serpent's neck.

Death by Piercing.

The serpent thrashed as my weapon pierced its scales. Its thrashing was so violent I was shaken off. I crashed onto the ground, my sword flying away and clattering to the floor. As I scrambled to my feet and raced toward my weapon, the enraged serpent turned to me and lunged forward. My life flashed before my eyes as it opened its mouth like it wanted to swallow me whole.

"Like I'd let you attack him!" Adina shouted as she burst forward like a speeding freight train.

She slammed a ball of energy into the serpent's head, and I was nearly blown back by the shockwave as the energy ball exploded. Light burst all around us, blinding in its brilliance, but I ignored that and reached for my sword. The by-now familiar hilt was comforting in my grip. Standing up, I turned to face the serpent, prepared to keep fighting… but I soon found out there was no need.

The serpent's head was missing.

It lay on the ground, twitching as though its muscles were spasming, but then it went still seconds later, and then it disappeared as the mana keeping it here evaporated.

"It seems you have gotten a lot stronger, Adina," Naamah shouted. She sounded angry. That made me chuckle. "However, do not think that growing a little stronger means you have what it takes to contend with me! I defeated your mother! I defeated Lilith!"

Adina snorted. "The only reason you beat Mother is because you, Agrat Bat Mahlat, and Eisheth Zenunim cavorted with Asmodeus to seal her away. You didn't defeat her in combat. You cowardly ganged up on her and used the powers of someone stronger than you to do what you couldn't!"

A loud snarl of rage resounded throughout the chamber. I looked around but still couldn't see where it was coming from. Fortunately, our resident archangel was now ready to unleash her spell.

Everything stood still as powerful waves of golden light spread across the room, all of them coming from Michelle, who emitted an energy so potent a shiver ran through my body. Adina also didn't seem to like this energy. She hid behind me as if the holy energy caused her pain. Meanwhile, a loud scream erupted from somewhere to my left.

It was Naamah. The woman was clawing at her face and screaming. I noticed smoke pouring off her face, so I guessed that spell Michelle unleashed did more than just dispel her illusion. Either way, this was an opportunity we couldn't afford to lose.

I raced forward, charging toward Naamah as fast as my legs could carry me. Footsteps echoed behind me. That must have been

Adina. I reached Naamah within several seconds and thrust my now glowing sword at her.

My Death by Piercing technique activated and my sword impaled the woman through the chest. A loud gasp escaped her lips, but she wasn't given time to properly feel the pain before I moved away and Adina flew forward. Her body spun through the air as she released a powerful heel kick. She didn't hit Naamah. She hit the sword in her chest. The attack was so powerful that Naamah was blasted off her feet, flew backward, struck the wall, and there she remained, her body sticking to the wall thanks to the sword impaling her chest.

And that was when Michelle used her next attack.

Sparks of golden electricity raced along her body, gathered around her hand, and then flew forward. They struck Naamah, whose shrieks of pain grew even louder. Sparks flew off her body as she threw her head back to howl out her pain. She didn't even notice her head striking the wall. She didn't notice the blood running down her face. The lightning fried her insides, causing smoke to pour from her mouth, nose, and ears. When the attack finally settled down, the woman remained where she was, her body still.

Adina walked up to her and began draining the woman of her life like she'd done for Maliperum. Meanwhile, I turned to Michelle.

"That attack was new," I said, raising an eyebrow.

Michelle shook her head. "It isn't a new attack. I've been able to use it this whole time, but I've never had a reason to. It is currently the most powerful attack in my arsenal." She glanced at Naamah as the woman's body disappeared, then sighed. "Of course, at its peak, that attack would have fried my enemy so badly their bodies would disintegrate."

I nodded as I checked my status and saw that our battle with Naamah had caused my level to increase by three whole levels. That woman must have been incredibly powerful to give me such a boost. I now had 30 status points and 6 skill points to spend. What's more, I had unlocked the ability to use several new skills, including Berserk, Dual-wielding, and the Shield skill.

The first thing I did was allocate my status points. After that, I selected the Dual-Wielding skill, which cost 10 skill points to activate. When I activated the Dual-Wielding skill, several new branches that had been grayed out suddenly appeared before me. I frowned at the new skills. All of them were related to my Dual-Wielding skill, meaning they were abilities I could use in conjunction with my new one.

Double Slash: The ability to unleash a powerful combination attack while dual-wielding two swords. Damage dealt is doubled upon successful attack. This attack is not as effective against heavily armored opponents.
Whirlwind Axel: An upgraded variation of Whirlwind Slash. Using two blades to spin on the balls of your feet, users can unleash a ferocious tornado-like force of energy that slices into multiple opponents at once.
Triple Thrust: Stab your opponent three times in rapid succession. Critical damage dealt. This attack has the chance of instantly killing any opponent whose level is lower than your own.

Each skill required one skill point to activate, and like my other skills, their strength could increase by allocating more skill points to them. After a moment, I activated Double Slash and Whirlwind Axel, then allocated the remaining points between them.

Now my stats looked something like this:

Name: Bryan Jenson
Class: Magic Swordsman

Level: 62
Magic: Red/fire
Attack: 150
Agility: 150
Defense: 140
Magic Defense: 140
Mana: 120
Total Status Points available: 0

Special Skills:
Whirlwind Slash: Attack +5
Death by Piercing: Attack +5
Fire Slash: Attack +5
Fireball: Attack +5
Dual-Wielding (passive skill)
Whirlwind Axel: Attack +4
Triple Thrust: Attack +4
Total Skill Points available: 0

As I finished allocating all my skill points and status points, Adina ran up to me and threw her arms around my neck. She sought out my lips for a passionate kiss. I barely had time to get my head on straight, but I did my best to kiss her back. Wrapping my arms around the succubus, I pulled her close, enjoying the way her barely clothed tits squished against my chest.

"That was amazing!" Adina said, not even bothering to contain her excitement. "The way you impaled Naamah on your sword gave me chills! The good kind of chills!"

I opened my mouth to speak again, to say something super witty, but then Adina shoved her tongue into my mouth for another enthusiastic kiss. Her tongue filled my mouth. It was a pretty incredible feeling.

"Are you two quite finished?" asked Michelle, hands on her lips.

I would have said something, but Adina still had her tongue in my mouth, swirled her tongue around to stir up the saliva we were sharing, and only then retracted her face from mine. A string of saliva connected us before it was cut by the distance. With a satisfied grin, the succubus stepped back.

"Don't worry. I'm done." She gestured toward Michelle. "You can have your turn now."

"Hmph."

Michelle released a huff, and I thought she was going to say something like angels didn't act so frivolously, but then she walked up to me and stopped just before entering my personal space. Her cheeks grew red as she looked at me. Crossing her arms, she turned her head.

"T-the man is supposed to take charge in situations like this," she muttered, which I guessed was her way of saying "I'd like to kiss you, but I don't want to admit it" or something similar to that.

"Right."

I chuckled as I placed my hands on her hips and drew her close. Michelle didn't resist as I leaned down and pressed our lips together. A sigh escaped her mouth as I applied a light pressure and nibbled on her lower lip. She gasped when I slipped my tongue inside of her, but then her own tongue tentatively rubbed against mine, sending electric arcs of pleasure through my body.

I think we would have stayed like this for awhile yet, but just as I was about to deepen our kiss further, a loud and surprised voice squawked from the other side of the chamber.

"W-what the fuck?! Bryan?!"

At the sound of the voice, Michelle leapt out of my arms. Adina and I turned to look at the source of the voice. Several people were standing near the secret passage where the imps, trolls, and succubi that Naamah had summoned emerged from during my first fight with her. There stood Elric, Vyra, Brad, and a woman I didn't know with bright blonde hair, large tits, and dressed in Viking-like armor.

"You guys are late. I already took care of our little succubus problem," I said to them, smiling at their stupefied expressions.

CHAPTER 10

We were sitting inside of the chamber where Adina, Michelle, and I had defeated Naamah. I was actually surprised by how easy it was. I'd been expecting a much harder fight, but maybe I only thought that way because of the first time I fought her alongside Brad, Elric, and Vyra. We had been only at level 50. Meanwhile, Michelle and I were quite a bit stronger now.

My sword was back in its sheath. I had to pry it out of the wall where Adina had kicked it. Speaking of, the two lovely non-human ladies were sitting on either side of me, facing the wary Brad, the grinning Elric, the scowling Vyra, and the curious blonde woman… whose name I still didn't know. I should really fix that.

"I knew you were still alive," Brad said with an expression that resembled admiration. "When we traveled out of the Rift Plains and logged out to get back to Earth, we noticed that you were still alive. All of your vitals were functioning and your brain activity was normal… well, relatively normal minus a lot of spikes in your pain receptors. However…" He glanced at Adina and Michelle, then chuckled. "I never expected this. You remind me of a friend I know. He also teamed up with an otherworldly being, though he did it to find his dead wife."

"Uh huh…" I didn't know what he was talking about, but I didn't think it was important. "Anyway, I think all of us need to get caught up on what everyone has been doing. I see you've got a new member on your team. Care to introduce us?"

"My name is Christine Douval," the blonde woman with massive mammaries introduced herself. I noticed that her skin was somewhat orange. At first, I thought it was a bad tan from a tanning booth, but the more I looked at it, the more certain I became that wasn't the case.

"Christine was one of the first people to enter the Rift Plains," Brad explained. "She's not an avatar like you or me. This is her physical body."

Christine nodded and explained further. "I stumbled upon a portal while I was working my dead-end job. I ended up in a strange world, and I probably would have died, but a group of women calling themselves Valkyries took me in and trained me. They taught me magic and how to fight, and they allowed me to Soul Bond with one of their worlds." She caressed the vambraces covering her arms and smiled as if remembering something pleasant. "Since then, I have been traveling through the numerous worlds in the Rift Plains and helping other people who have become stuck here."

"We actually stumbled on her by accident," Elric added. "We were arguing about how to go about rescuing you when she appeared before us and offered to help."

As he finished speaking, Vyra scowled. "Correction, we were trying to decide whether or not mounting a rescue mission was even worth it."

At those words, Michelle, who had been silent to this point, frowned. "You would leave a comrade behind?"

"It's not like I wanted to," Vyra groused, looking away from the archangel's stern expression. "But the chances of a successful rescue mission seemed pretty damn slim, especially after we got our asses kicked fighting that woman." She sighed. "Not that it matters now. Looks like you took care of the cunt."

"Damn right, we did," Adina cheered. "We beat Naamah good!"

"We've explained our situation to you," Brad suddenly said as he glanced at Adina. "Why don't you explain what happened after you were captured? I'm sure everyone would like to know."

It was a fair enough point. I did my best to explain how I'd been captured, tortured for information, and then worked with the two women beside me to escape. There were a few moments I left out, like how I had sex with them both. I didn't think that was important. After informing the group about what happened to me, I looked at Adina and Michelle.

"Care to introduce yourselves?" I asked.

"I am Michelle." The archangel went first, her head held high, chest thrust out. "I am an archangel of heaven, though I was expelled from heaven recently thanks to the rebellion that broke out when we angels gained free will."

"And I'm Adina!" The succubus raised her hand and gave them a broad smile. She seemed incredibly happy. "I'm the daughter of Lilith, Queen of the Succubus, and I'm Bryan's lover alongside Michelle!"

At the mention of being my lover, the four newcomers looked at me like they were seeing me for the first time. Brad was blinking like he didn't understand what Adina had said, Vyra's scowl had grown even deeper, Elric was giving me a discreet thumbs up, and Christine looked at me with undisguised interest within those deep cerulean eyes. Michelle was giving Adina the stink eye. Her cheeks were a light shade of pink.

"I thought we were going to keep silent on that," Michelle hissed.

"Were we?" Adina looked honestly confused. "No one said anything to me."

Michelle's response was to bury her face into her hands.

"So while you were trapped within this world, you picked up a pair of lovers?" Brad said in shock.

"Er... more or less," I admitted, not quite sure what else I could say now that the cat was out of the bag.

"Yup. You definitely remind me of my friend." Brad sighed and rubbed his forehead as if trying to rub out a headache.

I shrugged. I didn't know who his friend was, so I really couldn't say anything about that.

"In either event, now that you're here and you've defeated Naamah, we can continue to travel further into this world," Brad continued as he stood up. "This dungeon is just one small section of this world. Our goal is to completely clean out this world of all hostile forces, defeat the Dungeon Master, and become the master of this world."

"Right. You want to become the dungeon master," I said with a grunt as I stood to my feet.

Brad gave me a fierce grin. "You bet I do."

Everyone else also stood up. I helped Adina and Michelle to their feet. The people around me were getting ready to leave, hefting their equipment over their shoulders, making sure their weapons were secure, and checking their supplies. It looked like they had somehow brought equipment over. I wasn't sure how that worked, but maybe Christine had something to do with it.

However, just as we were getting ready to move out, a loud gurgling erupted all around us. Brad, Elric, Vyra, and even Christine moved into a combat stance as though expecting an enemy to ambush us. Michelle and I, however, looked at Adina. The succubus was holding her stomach, tail hanging limply from her body as she stood with a slouched posture.

"Erm… do any of you have food?" she asked sheepishly. "I'm really hungry."

Her words caused the four who'd come after we defeated Naamah to look at her like she'd just said something phenomenally stupid.

***

It turned out they did pack food into their belongings, or rather, Christine had brought food along with her. Because she was not an avatar but an actual person, she needed to eat in order to live.

I found it rather odd how I didn't seem to require food. While I could eat, and it did satisfy me, eating wasn't required for this body to survive. It was just another matter that caused a disconnect with this whole situation and made it seem like all this was just a game.

With Naamah's death, cleaning out the rest of this dungeon was an easy matter. We swept through it like a hurricane, defeating every demon within the dungeon.

Our levels didn't increase during this time. Well, mine, Michelle's, and Adina's didn't increase at all. I wasn't sure about Brad, Christine, Elric, and Vyra. I didn't even know what their levels were. However, I wasn't sure ours could increase from fighting such weak creatures anymore. It was just like Adina and Michelle said: The higher a person's level became, the harder it was for them to level up.

After what felt like several hours of tedious work, our group finally arrived at what looked like the entrance to a crypt. A pair of pillars stood on either side of a dark entrance. The stone walls appeared old, cracked and crumbling in places, and a cold breeze blew in from the dark opening, causing goosebumps to appear on my arms.

"We'll rest here for now," Brad announced. "The demons in this lower level are much stronger than the ones we've been fighting up to now. We should use this time to prepare ourselves."

As he spoke, everyone branched off into groups and sat down. Vyra and Christine sat together, having seemingly grown close during the time I wasn't around, and Elric sat with them. It looked like he was trying to hit on Christine without success. The woman politely but firmly rebuffed all of his attempts. Despite this, the man did not give up and kept trying. I would have admired his persistence, but I felt like he was annoying the two women.

Brad stood alone in front of the cave entrance, his serious expression making it look like his face was carved from stone. I wondered what he was thinking. To be honest, I still knew next to nothing about this guy beyond the fact that he knew a lot more about the Rift Plains than most people and was probably loaded with money.

Michelle and Adina sat next to me as I leaned against the wall. Adina, being the more affectionate of the two, was resting her head on my shoulder. Michelle was not doing that. However, she had discreetly reached out to grab my arm. I think she was too embarrassed to do anything more in front of so many people.

"I've been thinking," Adina said.

"That doesn't sound good," Michelle quipped.

Adina stuck out her tongue before continuing. "This body of yours is just an avatar, right? The real you isn't here?"

"That's right." I nodded. "My real body is currently hooked up to a super high-tech virtual reality rig that lets me travel to the Rift Plains."

Nodding, Adina's nose wiggled a little. It was such a cute gesture from the sexy succubus that I felt warmth fill my chest. As she leaned further into me, her breasts squished against my arm, allowing me to feel the wonderful elasticity of her tits.

"That means me and Michelle haven't actually had sex with the real you since that isn't your real body." Adina pouted up at me. "I'm rather upset by this fact."

Leave it to a succubus to be upset by the fact that she had sex with an avatar body and not my real body. On the other side, Michelle's face took on a strange expression like she was thinking about something really hard, while also trying not to blush.

"There isn't much I can do about that right now," I admitted with a smile.

"I know," Adina said morosely.

"Since this is not your real body, I have to wonder what will happen after all this," Michelle suddenly said. When Adina and I looked at her, she cast her gaze at me, her complex expression containing numerous mixed emotions. "Once we have secured this world and your friend becomes the master of it, what will happen to us? You are going to travel back to your world, right? Back to your real body on Earth? That means you won't be here anymore."

Now that she had spoken her thoughts, I could see the worry contained in her face, the uncertainty. It was surprising that she would worry about this so much. At the same time, it did make me happy that she was worrying about this. It meant she was serious about our relationship.

I placed a hand on her thigh and gave it a reassuring squeeze. "You don't have to worry about that. It is true that I'll need to return to my body, but that doesn't mean I plan on disappearing. Christine said she arrived on the Rift Plain by stumbling through a portal back on Earth. That means if I can find a portal, I can come back."

"You'd do that?" asked Adina, leaning forward even more, eyes containing a fervent glow like they contained all her hope. "You would leave your world for us?"

Gazing at Adina's pink lips caused my mouth to go dry. If I wasn't surrounded by other people, I would have kissed her. Smiling instead, I gave her a firm nod.

"I have nothing tying me down back on Earth," I admitted. "I haven't spoken to my family in years. I don't have anyone waiting for me. Ever since my best friend died, I've been living, but I was never really alive." I chuckled a little, but it sounded self-deprecating to my ears. "It might seem weird, but coming to this world and meeting you two has been the best thing that ever happened to me."

Adina's eyes glowed as a smile caused her beautiful lips to curl delightfully, and even Michelle looked happy with my words. I smiled too—or I tried to. Before my lips could fully form one, Adina lunged forward and planted a kiss on my mouth. I groaned as she pushed her tongue inside of my mouth, creating a ceaseless friction as she rubbed our tongues together. When she leaned back, slowly extracting her tongue from my mouth, a string of saliva connected us until she broke it with a swipe of that fleshy pink appendage.

I was a bit dazed from the kiss. Adina was not as she gazed into my eyes and smiled.

"When you get here in your real body, we are going to have a lot of sex."

"Uh… yeah, sure," I agreed with a nod. I wasn't against having sex, but I still felt like my brain had melted through my ears, so that was about all I could say.

Michelle glared at us, and I thought she was angry at first, but the more I thought about it, the more I realized she was probably jealous. As my mind returned from limbo, I leaned over to her and placed a kiss on her sweet lips. She was startled at first. Yet as I let my mouth linger on hers, she closed her eyes and leaned forward.

As I leaned away from Michelle, who had closed her eyes, I realized several eyes were on us. I turned my head. Christine, Elric, and Vyra were staring. While Vyra wore her typical scowl, Christine looked like she was observing us with keen interest. I wondered what sort of thoughts were going through her head. On the other hand, Elric was giving me a thumbs up. I really did worry about that guy sometimes.

"It's time to go," Brad said, turning around and gazing at us. "Everyone, let's pack up and move out."

We all stood up and moved toward the entrance. I peered down as the cold breeze blowing up from this dark staircase hit me in the face. There were no lanterns or torches or anything to light our path. As I wondered how we'd get down without falling, Michelle created a light sword that provided some illumination. Then Christine also created a ball of light that floated gently above her palm. This ball of light created a bright glow that banished the darkness and allowed everyone to see the stone steps leading down.

"Let's go," Brad said as he began walking down the stairs.

The rest of us followed him, our footsteps causing staccato echoes to bounce back to us. I had no idea how far down this staircase went. Adina didn't know either. Despite being a succubus like her brethren, she had never been down this way. According to her, Naamah had guarded this entrance zealously.

As we walked, Elric suddenly came up to my side. Adina and Michelle moved to the front. I didn't know if they were giving us privacy to talk or if they wanted privacy for some girl talk. However, they walked over to Christine and began speaking with her, so I assumed they had something they wished to discuss with the woman.

"I'm really glad to see you're not dead," Elric said suddenly. "I was pretty worried about you. When you suddenly collapsed after allowing us to break free, I tried to go back, but…"

"It's a good thing you didn't go back," I said with a shrug. "You would have just been captured alongside me. That wouldn't have done any good for anyone."

"I know." Elric was silent for a moment, his eyes traveling to Adina and Michelle. A hint of lust appeared in his gaze. He turned back to look at me with a salacious grin. "Though now I'm kinda wishing I was the one who got kidnapped. I think it would be worth it to have two hot lovers, and to think they're both so different." He sighed wistfully. "An angel and a succubus. What a combination."

I smiled despite myself. "You can't have them."

"I wasn't gonna ask if you'd share or anything!"

I chuckled just a little. Elric and I weren't what I would call friends, but he was probably the person I was closest to back in our world. He was the only one who still spoke to me.

My parents didn't call, and I didn't bother calling them. I suppose you could say we were estranged. They didn't approve of my desire to join the military. I still remember how they kicked me out after I graduated from high school, telling me that if I joined the military, they would disavow me and never let me return home. At the time, I had been so enraged that I left and never looked back.

I wondered what they were doing now? Probably getting by just fine without me.

We reached the end of the staircase eventually, and I nearly tripped as the area around us expanded, revealing a massive room filled with stone coffins. It looked like this place really was some kind of crypt. The stone floor had several symbols carved into it. I glanced at the nearest wall, upon which a relief of a woman bleeding from a chest wound as a knife pierced her heart was engraved. Several columns lined this room, traveling up to the ceiling, which contained a series of complex lattice work.

"I do not like the look of this place," Adina murmured as she traveled away from Christine and over to me. Michelle was trailing behind her, eyes warily glancing at the coffins.

"There is a dark energy emitting from this place," the archangel said. "I sense the power of death hanging heavily over this crypt."

"I'm guessing that's not a good thing," I said.

Michelle shook her head. "No, it is not. There are many malevolent spirits down here, and all of them are fairly powerful, though Naamah was stronger. However, I believe the further down we go, the more dangerous and more powerful our enemies will become."

I nodded to show her I understood, but we both knew there was nothing we could do about that. We really had no choice since we agreed to join Brad and his party. Reaching the final boss who controlled this world and becoming the dungeon master was the entire point in coming here.

As we walked passed the many coffins lining this room in rows of six, we came upon several other passageways. Each passage was marked by an entrance made from columns and an arched ceiling. There were four in total. All of them looked the same, which made choosing a path difficult.

"Do you think we should split up?" Elric asked Brad.

"No…" Brad shook his head. "We have no idea what sort of enemies are down here. Splitting up right now will divide our fighting force, which I don't think we can afford to do. Let's start from the left. We'll go down one path. If it turns out to be the wrong one, then we'll come back and travel down the next path until we find the right one."

"I have a very bad feeling about this," Vyra muttered, the scowl on her face increasing as the claws on her hands extended and retracted.

"Do not worry," Christine assured the woman. "Even if we face powerful enemies down here, I am confident in my ability to deal with them."

I still didn't know how powerful Christine was, but she had mentioned she was Soul Bound to a world within the Rift Plains. She had also been trained by Valkyries, which I recognized from Norse mythology as the all-female caste of warriors under the direct command of Odin, though that was sadly the extent of my knowledge. Most of what I knew came from video games and pop culture. I didn't think Marvel's version of Odin was all that accurate to the actual mythology.

Under Brad's instructions, our group traveled down the leftmost passage, which narrowed into another hallway. With Michelle's and Christine's light illuminating the area around us, I was able to look at the stone walls. I found a crack on the wall to my left, which traveled from the bottom to the top before disappearing. Glancing forward, I looked at Brad, Christine, Elric, and Vyra as they warily eyed their surroundings.

This passage didn't branch off into multiple directions. We eventually reached the end, which opened into a massive cavern space with a lake, of all things. It didn't look like there was anything else. Elric stepped up to the shores of the lake. The murky black water looked incredibly foul as it lapped at the rocky shore.

"It doesn't look like this is the right way," Elric said as he turned around. "Let's head back."

Brad nodded. "We'll try the next passage."

Before we could leave, the water several yards from the shore bubbled. It was the only warning we received before a black shadow shot from the water and grabbed onto Elric's leg, hauling him off the ground. Elric screamed in fear as the object, which I now recognized was a tentacle, vigorously shook him back and forth. Meanwhile, several more tentacles erupted from the water and came at us.

"Damn it!" I swore as I pulled my sword from my sheath.

Everyone else readied their weapons as well. When the tentacles came at us, I dodged to the side and used Fire Slash to hack the tentacle off. As the tentacle fell to the ground, thrashing about like it was still alive, I moved away and closer to Adina, who slammed her fist into another one of the tentacles, which undulated underneath her powerful punch. However, it looked like this thing was resistant to blunt force damage. I spun around and swung my blade upward, hacking off that tentacle too.

"Thanks for that," Adina said as she pressed her back against mine.

"You're welcome," I responded.

The others weren't sitting idle while I'd been attacking. Vyra was slashing away at the tentacles with her powerful claws. She flapped her wings and flew into the air before descending and slamming her clawed feet slammed into one of the tentacles, crushing it beneath her feet and creating cracks in the ground. Then she used her impressive draconic strength to dig her claws into the tentacle and tore it off. Following this, as what remained of the tentacle tried to retract, Vyra opened her mouth and unleashed a powerful blaze that consumed the tentacle and turned it to ash.

Damn. I hadn't realized the woman could breathe fire like a real dragon. That was actually pretty cool.

As I was admiring the fire breathing Vyra, an orange light suddenly engulfed my body, and a rush of energy spread through me. I blinked as any and all fatigue vanished. I felt... strong. I felt like I could easily take on the entire world right now. This confused me, but then I saw Christine standing back and waving her sword, from which the orange light spread and engulfed myself and the others.

I see. This woman had some kind of magic that boosted our physical abilities.

With our strength suddenly increased, all of us rushed forward and hacked into the tentacles. Michelle swung her sword left and right as she elegantly danced across the ground. Several tentacles fell before the might of her swings. Black blood sprayed from the stumps, splattering against the ground. She was like an angel of death.

While we were battling against the tentacles, Elric managed to free himself by bashing his glowing mace against the tentacle holding him. He fell into the water with a splash, then tried to swim to shore, though I had no idea how he didn't sink with that paladin armor on.

As he was trying to get to the shore, something large appeared behind him. It had a bulbous head, large black eyes, and a gaping maw filled with row upon row of sharp teeth. I couldn't tell what this creature was, though I was vaguely reminded of this movie I saw about a monster called a kraken. A loud sucking sound emerged from its mouth as the monster tried to inhale Elric, who slowly began getting sucked toward its mouth.

"Holy shit, you guys! This thing is trying to eat me! A little help here?!"

Brad wore a grim expression as he hacked off several tentacles with his scythe and rushed forward. Black fire spread along his scythe as he raced across the water like he was gliding. I wondered how he was doing that, but I knew now was not the time to contemplate such things. As I hacked off more tentacles, Brad finally made it to the creature and sliced into one of its eyes with his scythe.

"SCREEE!!!!"

Vyra and Adina dropped to their knees and covered their ears as a piercing wail echoed from the creature.

Michelle grimaced, but unlike those two who seemed to have enhanced hearing, she didn't drop to her knees, and instead tossed her blade into the air. She caught it in her hand, but now she was holding it by the hilt like a football. A golden spark ran along the sword. One spark became two, two became three, and soon sparks covered the entire weapon.

With a grunt, Michelle threw the weapon like it was a javelin. It flew forward, a golden streak of light that left a trail in its wake, so fast I could barely see it. While I couldn't see the weapon as it moved, I did see the aftermath as it plunged into the monster in the lake. It stabbed the creature right between the eyes.

The pained shrieking grew weaker and weaker as the monster thrashed around. Elric, no longer being sucked into its mouth, swam as quickly as he could to the shore, gasping and heaving as he stumbled onto dry land. Meanwhile, the monster's thrashing lessened as it slowly sank into the depths of the lake.

"Was that the same attack you used to defeat Naamah?" I asked.

"It was," Michelle admitted. "It can be used as either a ranged attack, or I can infuse a weapon with it and attack that way. It's quite versatile."

"I'll say," Adina said with a wistful sigh. "I wish I had a power like that, but I still haven't Soul Bound myself to a world."

"You could always Soul Bind to this world," Christine remarked.

Adina shook her head. "No thanks. If I'm going to Soul Bond with a world, I'd rather it be a red or pink world. We succubi are emotional creatures who rely on passion and lust to power us, so a world with the power of death would only hinder us in the long run."

Christine shrugged as though it didn't matter to her. While this conversation went on, I helped Elric to his feet. The man coughed and wheezed as I slung his arm around my shoulder and walked further from the lake. Brad also moved Elric's other side and helped me out.

"This way is definitely a dead end," Brad said. "Let's head back the way we came and try the next passage."

All of us agreed. However, as we began moving back down the passage that lead back to the crypt, I couldn't help but worry about what sort of dangers we would uncover next.

CHAPTER 11

"Haaaaa!"

As I descended from the air, I swung the two swords fiercely gripped in my hands downward. Blood splashed against the ground as two thick lines were carved into the giant beast before me. The creature was massive but thin. It stood on two skinny legs, had feet the size of a human torso, and possessed a skinny torso that showed off its ribcage, and it carried a dagger in each hand. A head like a beast was matched with equally wild hair. Two horns jutted from this creature's head and curved backward.

Alaster was its name. These were the latest demons our group had run into, and they were quite powerful.

After carving a deep furrow into Alaster's chest, the creature stumbled backward but didn't fall. Rage made its eyes turned red as it glared at me. With a sound that was half-screech and half-roar echoing out of its mouth, it lunged toward me, dagger set to impale me.

"Not on my watch!!" Adina shouted as she leapt into the air, flapped her wings, and used her immense physical strength to punch Alaster's hand. A strange undulating ripple spread from the point of impact. This was followed by a loud *bang* as a shockwave spread out. So powerful was this shockwave that even I was pushed back a bit.

The arm that Adina punched slammed into the ground several feet to my left. I could see a large bruise had formed in the shape of her fist on Alaster's arm.

Before the creature had time to recover, Adina landed on its arm, raced up, and reared her fist back. Her next punch was simple, straightforward, and effective. It crashed into Alaster's face like a hurricane. Several teeth shattered, the shards littering the ground, and blood flew from its mouth. Now more pained than enraged, the demon howled as it stumbled back—right into Michelle.

Michelle had moved around to the back and attacked its legs. Her sword of light flashed out as she swung at speeds even I could not keep up with. Several incision lines appeared on Alaster's legs near the Achilles' heel, the back of the knee, and the quadriceps. Blood splattered against the stone floor as cuts burst open like overripe fruit being crushed by an iron fist. Its legs no longer able to bear its weight, the demon crashed to the ground, onto its hands and knees.

That was when I went for the finishing blow.

Triple Thrust.

I reached its head and thrust both swords out, first then left, then the right, and then the left again. Three times in quick succession my swords flashed out. The first attacked caused Alaster's left eye to burst. The second attacked caused the same to its right eye. My third attacked slipped between the eyes and punctured a hole through its skull. As I stepped back and sheathed both swords, I watched as the now eyeless, slack-jawed demon slumped face first to the ground.

It was over.

"We did it!" Adina cheered.

Michelle acted far more reserved, but even she smiled. "We are getting a lot stronger."

"Considering how powerful these demons are, we had better be getting stronger," I muttered as I wiped the sweat from my brow. Alaster burst into dust seconds after, and I heaved a sigh of relief. That had been an intense fight.

"What is your level at now?" Adina asked as she and Michelle walked over to me.

With a small sigh, I pulled up my status screen and checked to see my stats.

Name: Bryan Jenson
Class: Magic Swordsman
Level: 69
Magic: Red/fire
Attack: 170
Agility: 170
Defense: 140
Magic Defense: 140
Mana: 150
Total Status Points available: 0

Special Skills:
Whirlwind Slash: Attack +5
Death by Piercing: Attack +5
Fire Slash: Attack +5
Fireball: Attack +5
Dual-Wielding (passive skill)
Whirlwind Axel: Attack +10
Triple Thrust: Attack +10
Total Skill Points available: 0

"It looks like I haven't gone up from level 69 yet," I said with a small frown. I pulled up another screen and checked to see how much Life Essence I needed to reach my next level. "And it says I still need 4,569 Life Essence Points before I reach level 70." My frown grew. "That demon gave me a thousand points, but it's just not enough. I need to kill at least five more."

Michelle shrugged. "Such is the nature of increasing your level. The higher your level, the more Life Essence you need to reach the next one."

"I know," I said.

"Let's just keep working hard," Adina suggested.

Michelle gave Adina a scathing look. "It is easy for a succubus like you to say that. You can raise your level simply by sleeping with Bryan."

"Tee-hee!"

"Don't laugh like this is a joke!"

As Adina and Michelle began what I'd taken to calling their comedy routine, I looked at the others and saw they were all done with their fights. Elric, Vyra, and Christine had finished off the Alaster they'd been fighting. Meanwhile, Brad had taken care of all the smaller enemies that had surged around the two larger enemies' legs. The man in the dark black armor and wielding a scythe struck an awfully solemn figure as he stood there all by his lonesome.

"Honestly," Michelle sighed and placed a hand on her forehead. "I wish I could level up simply by having sex with Bryan. Life would be so much easier."

"But it's not like my level just increases, you know." Adina pouted, her cheeks swelling like a pair of balloons. "I can only use that method to increase my level to the level of whoever I am sleeping with. Once I'm at the same level as that person, I can't draw anymore Life Essence from them. And I haven't had to do that with Bryan since I already reached level 69." Adina placed her hands on her hips and thrust out her massive breasts, which jiggled and shook like a pair of water balloons. "I reached that level all on my own, you know."

"Maybe level 69, but I'm pretty sure you gained the previous two levels by sleeping with Bryan," Michelle said.

"Well… yes. That is true."

Adina rubbed the back of her head, while Michelle rolled her eyes and smirked. As they finished talking, the two walked with me over to where the others were all waiting. Michelle's toga swayed as she moved. Each step appeared incredibly elegant. Meanwhile, Adina walked with a bounce in her step and a sway in her hips, which caused her chest to jiggle uncontrollably. Adding to the sensual allure of her walk, her wings extended and retracted several times.

"Is anyone injured?" Brad asked, looking at all of us. When we shook our heads, he nodded. "Then let's move on."

We began walking again, following Brad as he led us through this labyrinth with a grim expression marring his face. This particular area looked a lot like a maze. There were many turns and dead ends and we even found ourselves walking in circles a number of times. Sometimes we would run into open rooms like this one, which were filled with demonic legions, but other times we would simply find ourselves going nowhere.

I wasn't sure how long we'd been down here. My internal clock had long since lost track of time. With no sunlight, no seasons, and nothing except my own sense of exhaustion to guide me, I couldn't figure out if days, weeks, or months had passed.

"You three are quite the team," Christine said as she walked up to us with a smile. "You took down that Alaster like it was nothing. I'm very impressed by how well-coordinated your attacks were."

"Thanks!" Adina said with a smile.

"You and your group are not bad either," Michelle added.

But Christine shook her head. "We don't work as well as you three. Your bonds are a lot stronger than ours. It allows you to really bring out the full potential of each member of your group."

"I suppose that is true," Michelle said with a slow nod as she glanced at Elric, who was speaking enthusiastically to the scowling Vyra. "Your other two teammates do not mesh well together, I have noticed."

"Elric is a pretty cheerful guy, but I think he grates on Vyra's nerves," Christine admitted with an amused smile.

"And you?" I asked curiously.

Christine tilted her head as she pondered the question, then shrugged. "I do not dislike him, but I do sometimes wish he would not hit on me. I'm not really here to find love."

"And what are you here for?" I asked.

"To stop this invasion from spreading." Christine shrugged. "The Rift Plains are currently on the brink of being completely overrun by powerful beings from numerous other worlds. If these creatures make it to the Rift Plains, they will have access to many portals that lead to Earth, and then they will come and many people will die." Christine's grim countenance made me frown. "I am sure you've noticed, but while some of the beings from this side are benevolent and kind . . ." She nodded at Adina and Michelle, who both smiled back. ". . . Even more of them are cruel and would gladly slaughter or enslave humanity for their own amusement."

"I have noticed that, yes," I said, thinking back to our battles against Maliperum and Naamah, two demons who epitomized what she was talking about.

"I don't want to see that happen." Christine's smile was filled with determination. "While I have chosen to stay in the Rift Plains, I do have family living back on Earth, and I don't wish to see them be enslaved or killed."

Everyone had a motivation for doing something, whether it was fame, fortune, glory, or to protect the people they cared about. My original reason for agreeing to help Brad was simple. I wanted to escape. I wanted to run away from the haunting nightmares that plagued me, to escape from my inescapable past, if only for a little while. My reasons weren't anywhere close to being noble like Christine's were.

It really made me think.

We continued on for what felt like several hours, stopped when we became hungry, slept when we became tired, and fought when we ran into enemies.

Alaster was a fairly rare—and exceptionally powerful—demon that only showed up occasionally, like once every few days. Most of the creatures were fought were demons like Lamia and Incubus.

Lamia were harmful spirits who killed infants and seduced sleeping men. There were a lot of rumors surrounding these vengeful spirits back in my world. One story said that Lamia was originally the queen of Libya, daughter of Belus and Libya, who won Zeus's heart. In her jealousy, Hera killed all of Lamia's children who were fathered by Zeus, and when Lamia retreated to a cave, she unleashed her wrath by killing the offspring of human mothers, usually by sucking the blood of the children.

She was also sometimes associated with Adam's first wife, Lilith, but Adina assured me that whoever came up with that particular story was an idiot and didn't know what they were talking about. What I did know was that her name was derived from a female demon with dragon heads at the end of their feet. Whatever they were, these vicious demons looked like hags with long noses, dried leather skin, and were covered in large cloaks that hid their decaying, wretched bodies.

By contrast, Incubi were much more simple to understand. They looked mostly human. However, their skin was sometimes a different color—mostly red and pink—and they had the appearance of fallen angels with wings blacker than the night sky and glowing red eyes. They were also naked. None of them wore a single stitch of clothing, which meant their nut sacks were out for everyone to see. I still remember the first time we had run into one and Michelle used her sword to relieve the demon of its cock.

I had felt equal parts vindication and sympathy.

As the hours—or days?—passed, our group eventually arrived at a large door. Though I called it large, I think massive might have been a better descriptor, for this door was so huge that it disappeared high above us. Darkness engulfed the area above our heads, so I couldn't even see where the door ended. Made from a green metal of some manner, the door contained the depiction of a demon with the heads of a ram, a bull, and a man. His body looked like a mishmash of animal parts. What's more, this creature was feasting on a naked human woman.

I felt my lips curl in disgust.

"This is a relief of Asmodeus," Michelle stated as she looked distastefully at the door. "There is a story about him. He once tormented Raguel's daughter, Sarah, killing off each husband she wed before they could have intercourse. After the seventh husband died, Sarah was about to hang herself in grief, but instead prayed to God for death. He answered her prayer by sending Raphael to aid her. He instructed Tobiah to place a fish liver and heart on the embers for incense, which repelled Asmodeus when he appeared to claim her next husband." She paused for a moment, then clicked her tongue. "I somehow doubt Raphael would come to that girl's aid again."

From her bitter words, I got the feeling Raphael was now one of the bad guys, a member of the group who had expelled her from Heaven.

"We will rest here for now," Brad said at last. "It looks like we are almost finished with this mission. I don't want anything bad to happen because we got overconfident and attacked before we were ready."

No one disagreed with his words. Soon, all of us had found a spot to rest.

The current area around us looked a lot like the ruins of an ancient civilization, complete with debris littering the ground, decayed walls that were crumbling in numerous places, and fallen columns that had tipped over. It was a wide space as well. Everything here looked a lot bigger than anything I had ever seen back on Earth. It looked like this place had been made for giants.

I sat with my back resting against one of the pillars, eating a light meal of dried meat. It wasn't much, but I was only eating because it was a habit. I didn't actually need to eat.

Adina and Michelle sat with me, as always.

The cuddly succubus was hugging my left right close as she leaned her head on my shoulder. Her tail had curled around one of my legs and was affectionately stroking it. Fortunately, her wings had retracted, so they weren't getting in the way.

Michelle sat on my other side, so close our thighs were touching. She quietly ate her meal of dried meat without complaint. As she ate, her robes shifted every so often to showcase her ample assets. When I looked at her, my eyes ended up traveling down until they reached her pale thighs, which were visible because her toga was riding up her legs.

"I want to have sex," Adina suddenly said.

Michelle rolled her eyes. "When don't you want to have sex?"

"Heh heh. Never." Adina giggled as though she'd told a joke. "But seriously. We haven't been able to have sex for awhile now. I really wish we could sneak off and at least get in a quicky."

"Nothing is ever quick with you," I said with a snicker. "There's a time and place for everything, and now is not the time or place for sex."

While Adina pouted at me, Michelle nodded. "I agree with Bryan. We are currently on the cusp of our most important battle to date. Beyond those gates lies a demon even some of Heaven's best warriors fear fighting. Asmodeus is not someone we can take on without being fully rested."

"I guess so," Adina said with a sigh. "In that case, I am going to sleep."

"Rest well," I said.

"Yeah…"

Adina shut her eyes and quickly drifted off, her breathing evening out and her tail going limp. She snuggled a little closer, nuzzling her nose against my shoulder and mumbling a bit before falling deeper into sleep. I remained still and tried not to shift. I didn't want her suddenly waking up. On my other side, Michelle released a soft sigh and smiled.

"That girl lives completely in the moment." Her smile turned brittle. "I wish I could do that."

"Are you thinking about your comrades up in Heaven?" I asked.

Reluctantly, she nodded. "I wish I could know what was happening up there, but even if I manage to escape from this world, I do not know which portal leads to my Heaven. It's something of an oddity, but there are dozens or perhaps even hundreds of different heavens, and each one is a little different. Anyway, when I was expelled, it was incredibly violent and I had no time to figure out where I was. All I could do was run away."

"I'm sure you'll be able to return eventually," I assured her. "We will be with you every step of the way."

"Thank you," Michelle murmured.

I smiled. "Get some sleep."

With a slow nod, Michelle yawned before making herself comfortable, which meant placing her head on my lap. I wondered if she realized she was acting so intimately with me in front of everyone else. Perhaps she was too tired. She slowly closed her eyes and drifted off to sleep. Since I still wasn't tired, I spent my time gently running my free hand through her hair, until even I was too tired to stay awake and drifted off.

"Hey, Bryan. You and your lovely ladies need to get up now."

I jerked awake at the sound of the voice, blinking my eyes open as something stirred on my leg.

Looking down, I saw Michelle slowly waking up, lifting her head off my leg as she glanced around with an expression that made her seem as groggy as I felt. A little bit of drool was leaking from her mouth. For whatever reason, I thought it was adorable. Michelle's pure white wings flapped a little as she continued waking up, and I turned my attention to Adina. The succubus sleeping against my shoulder was a much heavier sleeper than Michelle. She was pressed firmly into me, her well-developed and luscious body giving me thoughts of giving her the most orgasmic wake up of her existence, though I knew I couldn't do that here.

"We'll be up in just a moment," I finally said, looking at Elric.

"Yeah, sure. Hurry up, though. Brad is getting impatient," Elric said before wandering off toward the dark knight in all black.

"Time to get up, you two," I said to Michelle and Adina.

"I am already up," Michelle groaned as she placed a hand on her head. "Though I really wish I was not."

"Is my lap that comfortable?" I asked as I shook Adina awake. The succubus squinted her eyes open as she peered at me and Michelle while smacking her lips. I gazed at those lips, wishing I could feel them wrapped around my cock, but only for a moment before I shook the thought away. Now wasn't the time.

The three of us stood up, Adina raising her arms and stretching out. I heard a number of loud pops from her back and shoulders, which made me wince, but she didn't seem to notice as a slight smile adorned her pretty face. She brought her arms back down and looked at the two of us.

"So, we're about to begin?" she asked.

I nodded. "Looks like we're heading into Asmodeus's lair."

"Fuuuun," Adina said with a drawl.

"I'm not sure what's so fun about it," Michelle muttered as she crossed her arms.

"That was sarcasm."

"Your sarcasm needs work."

As the two lightly bickered, we wandered over to where Brad, Christine, Elric, and Vyra were now standing. When they saw us coming, Brad and Christine smiled, Elric grinned, and Vyra scowled at us. I didn't let that bother me. Vyra was always scowling. I figured it was her default face, or maybe her reptilian features just made it seem like she could only scowl.

"Are we ready?" I asked as the three of us stopped alongside the others.

"We are," Brad confirmed. "All we need to do now is get this door open."

"Right. So, uh, just how are we supposed to get this door open?" Elric glanced at the massive door, easily twenty or thirty times bigger than us, with an uncertain look. "I mean, this thing is huge. Even with all of us pushing on it, I doubt this door will even budge."

The man had a point. As I gazed at the door, even I could not help but think opening it on our own would be impossible.

"Maybe there's some kind of lever or pulley that we can use," Vyra suggested with her typical scowl. She crossed her arms, a single clawed finger tapping against her hard scales. "A door like this would normally have some manner of opening it that doesn't require manpower."

"You mean it normally does in our world," Christine corrected with a shake of her head. "Do not forget that we're not on Earth anymore. Our world's logic doesn't necessarily apply to this one. What's more, I don't see any pulleys, levers, or anything that might suggest this door can be opened."

"Then what should we do?" asked Vyra.

Before anyone could propose another idea, the doors opened on their own, releasing a loud squeal as if the hinges were rusted over. All of us turned to look at the door. A pensive expression flashed across Vyra's and Christine's faces when they saw what was happening, and I couldn't blame them. It seemed like we were being invited inside, but considering who we believed was on the other side, it was clearly a trap.

"It looks like we've been offered an invitation," Brad said with a nervous chuckle. "It would be rude to refuse."

No one laughed.

We journeyed passed the doors, which had only opened a crack, but that was a big enough crack that all of us could walk through. The moment each of us had entered, the doors slammed shut. We were officially trapped.

The air inside of this place was incredibly stale and moldy. It was like the scent of decay and rotting flesh. As we walked further into the room, I could see that this place was truly massive. It vaguely reminded me of a colosseum. Several tiers encircled this room, though it didn't look like they were seats so much as layers of bedrock. I looked up. The ceiling high above us was visible thanks to a series of glowing crystals hanging from it. One of those crystals was bigger than the rest. When I glanced at it, I saw…

"Mother!!" Adina screamed as she tried to run forward, but Michelle stopped her, grabbing the girl by the hand to keep her from traveling too far ahead of them. "What are you doing, Michelle?! Let me go! My mother! She's right there!"

There was indeed a woman trapped inside that crystal, beautiful beyond compare, with succulent breasts that possessed beautiful pink nipples. Her skin was almost pure red, but her long hair was pink. Like all high-level succubus, this one had wings, a tail, and horns. Her horns were jutting from the side of her head and curved around the front to form something that resembled a tiara. Likewise, the end of her tail was shaped like a crown. Her exposed pussy was completely bare. It looked like whoever had trapped her inside wanted her to be in as humiliating a position as possible.

"You can't!" Michelle snapped. "If you go over there, you'll just die! Look!" Michelle pointed at something with her free hand. "Our enemy is right there waiting for us!"

Adina stopped struggling and brought her gaze down. Michelle was right. In the very center of this room, sitting on a throne made of skulls and bones, was a creature so massive I could tell even from this distance that he was at least taller than a three or four-story house. His skin was a combination of blistering red and black, but it didn't look like normal skin. It more closely resembled segmented armor made from dragon scales. Like the engraving on the door, this creature had three heads. None of his heads really looked human, but the most humanlike one sat between his shoulders on a normal neck. His shoulders were composed of his other two heads. His left head looked like a bull and his right a ram. With his massively clawed hands resting on the arms of his throne, this creature exuded a foul, potent energy of death and lust, which washed over us.

Swordsman of the Rift   178

"**It seems I finally have guests,**" Asmodeus said, and his voice was a bass rumble that shook the entire room and caused my bones to vibrate. "**How delightful. I have long wondered when all of you would finally arrive. Ever since my connection to Naamah was cut, I knew it was only a matter of time before you came to see me.**"

"Let go of my mom!" Adina shouted, her rage and sorrow mixing in her voice.

Asmodeus's deep, throaty chuckle caused the hairs on my arms to prickle. "**I absolutely will not. Your mother is the greatest trophy in my possession. The Succubus Queen Lilith. She is a fine trophy to display, is she not?**"

Adina shrieked and tried to race toward Asmodeus, but Michelle and I held her back. We couldn't afford to make any careless mistakes here.

"You are the master of this world, right?" Brad asked as he took a step forward. "The one in control?"

"**Hmph. That's correct, little one. I'm guessing you came here to try and steal this world from me. Most unfortunate. Fools like you will never amount to much. You're always biting off more than you can chew.**"

At that moment, Asmodeus stood up, and I finally realized that he was far, *far* bigger than I first thought. He towered over us. I remembered my parents telling me a story once called David and Goliath. It was a Christian story, ironically enough, about a young boy named David who fought against the giant Goliath. David manages to kill Goliath by slinging a rock at him. Sadly, I didn't think we would have that kind of windfall.

He took a step forward, his reverse-jointed leg slamming into the ground. I noticed there was a tail behind him. It swept over the ground, creating gale force winds that I could feel even from far away. He reached out a single arm, clad in strange red armor, and wrapped his fingers around the hilt of a massive sword that was leaning against the throne.

The sword was more vicious than anything I had ever seen. It didn't even look like a real functioning sword. The blade was made of what appeared to be the remains of demonic creatures. I could see tentacles, arms, and even eyes located within the blade. The jagged edges gave it a terrifyingly demonic feel, while the crossguard curved out from between the hilt and blade, creating a pair of nasty-looking pincers.

Of course, what really made this weapon seem so terrifying was definitely the eye in the center of the guard. A single demonic red eye with a black slit running down the middle looked around, eying us as though it was alive. Strange fires danced within it. If I looked closely enough, I could see tormented faces howling inside of the eye as if they were trapped souls damned to an eternity of suffering.

The atmosphere around us grew overbearingly tense as strange energy undulations wafted off Asmodeus's body. This power caused my knees to buckle. The others didn't look much better off. Brad was sweating, Christine's face was pale, Elric looked like he was about to vomit, and Vyra's entire body had grown tense. Adina and Michelle, my two lovers, wore grave expressions as the blood drained from their faces.

"It has been so long since I've had a good fight," Asmodeus admitted as he swung his blade, creating a powerful gust of wind that nearly knocked us off our feet. He peeled his lips back into a feral grin, revealing sharp and saw-like teeth. **"I hope you do not disappoint me."**

CHAPTER 12

The battle began when Asmodeus swung the massive sword in his hand, though I think it was more like a disgusting slab of body parts melded together…

"Everyone scatter!" Brad shouted before putting words into action.

All of us bolted away. Adina, Michelle, and Vyra flapped their wings and soared out of the strike zone, while those of us unfortunate enough to not have wings were forced to travel on foot.

I ran like hell as the sword came down, the air shrieking as it was cut. It happened in an instant. The sword slammed into the ground, and an incredible shockwave spread out from the point of impact. Myself, Brad, Christine, and Elric were struck hard by the explosive force, which rolled across the area like a powerful rippling shockwave. Pain seared into my side as my feet were lifted off the ground, and I was tossed through the air.

"Bryan!"

Two voices shouted before two pairs of arms grabbed onto me. I felt a moment of weightlessness before a powerful jerk set my shoulders ablaze. Looking up, I found Adina and Michelle flying away with me.

"You two…"

"Are you okay?" asked Adina.

"I'm fine, but…"

I looked back down at the ground, at where Asmodeus's sword even now lay embedded into the floor. As the demon pulled his sword away, I saw how it had left a massive trench in the ground. Cracks spread from this trench. They weren't tiny either, but large chasms that looked like you could fall down them and never reach the bottom.

"I had no idea Asmodeus would be this powerful," Michelle mumbled.

"No kidding," Adina added. "That was some swing."

"Yeah, well, you two had better get ready because he's coming back for his second swing," I warned them.

Asmodeus turned around to face us, his eyes glowing with malevolence, lips twisted into a sneer as he brought up his sword and swung it again. The power behind his swing was such that we felt the air pressure before his attack even reached us.

Adina and Michelle were quick to fly into a series aerial maneuvers. They dropped swiftly, losing altitude so the sword could pass over our heads, but even though it didn't hit us, the power behind that swing sent us spiraling out of control. The two girls screamed as we were forced into a sickening tailspin that caused the world around me to blur. I felt their hands let go of me and fell to the ground.

I think I was fortunate we were already so close to the ground. I landed on my ass, but it wasn't a far drop, and I quickly scrambled to my feet. Looking around for a moment, I found Adina and Michelle. The archangel was nearest to me, a little off to my left, rubbing her backside as she stood up. Adina was on my right. She was still on the ground and rubbing her head.

"You two okay?" I asked as I reached my hand out to Adina.

"I am fine," Michelle said.

"Me too," Adina assured me as she grabbed my hand.

"Good." I pulled the succubus to her feet as Michelle joined us. Then I looked at Asmodeus. "Now what are we going to do about that?"

Asmodeus was currently locked in combat against Brad, Christine, Elric, and Vyra, though it looked more like a couple of gnats buzzing around an annoyed human. Vyra was attacking from the sky, unleashing her powerful dragon's breath to no effect. Down below, Brad and Elric tried to take out Asmodeus's legs with their death and holy powers respectively. Christine was further back. It looked like she was using her powers to boost everyone's physical abilities.

As we watched, Asmodeus impaled his sword into the ground. Nothing seemed to happen at first, but then black flames erupted from around the sword, causing the stone floor to rupture. I could feel the heat even from here. I couldn't imagine how hot it was when you were right next to it.

Brad, Christine, and Elric were forced to move fast to avoid being incinerated. The flames continued to spread out. They did eventually stop, however, showing that there was a limit to the area of effect. Meanwhile, Vyra was swatted out of the sky when Asmodeus whacked her with a powerful backhand.

"Adina!"

"On it!"

As Vyra soared through the air like a rocket, Adina blasted off the ground and intercepted the woman before she could strike the hard wall. Both Vyra and Adina sailed through the air. However, Adina was physically the strongest out of all of us, and she stopped mere feet from striking the wall. I sighed in relief as Adina quickly floated back to the ground.

"Michelle! Let's go and distract Asmodeus! Maybe if we fight him, we'll discover his weakness!"

"I'm really not hopeful of that, but I suppose it is better than nothing."

Michelle took to the sky while I ran along on the ground. The chasm from Asmodeus's sword was before me, but I used the strength granted by my level 69 stats to leap clear over it. I landed on the ground and continued running.

Asmodeus was right in front of me, but Michelle had begun her attack, so he was a little busy. Bolts of golden lightning shot from her palms and slammed into the demon. I was surprised to see her attacks actually did damage, but I guess holy attacks were strong against demons like him. Even though Asmodeus had a weakness to holy damage, though the attacks still only caused small black scorch marks to appear on his skin.

"Ha ha ha! What is the matter, archangel?! Is that all you have?! Oh, how the mighty have fallen!"

From the grave scowl on Michelle's face, I could tell Asmodeus had hit a sore spot. She still wasn't at the level she had been before she was kicked out of Heaven.

Rather than make her feel weak, Asmodeus's words served to fuel her, and Michelle darted in close to his face, so close he couldn't attack her without the risk of hurting himself. I saw a flash of light. Then Asmodeus screamed in agony and rage as he stumbled backward. His free hand went up to his eye. I couldn't see what kind of damage was done, but I could at least assume his eye was a major weak point for him.

Unfortunately, this attack didn't just hurt him. It also enraged him. Asmodeus swung his sword at Michelle, who was able to dodge, but she couldn't avoid the air pressure from the swing. Astonishingly powerful gale winds slammed into Michelle, who spiraled and would have crashed to the ground had I not leapt up and caught her in my arms. I grimaced as her weight sent us both down. Landing on the stone floor, I bent my knees and skidded for several feet before stopping.

"You okay?" I asked.

"Yes," Michelle said, opening the eyes she had inadvertently closed. "I am all—look out!"

I looked up just in time to see a shadow closing in. It was Asmodeus's sword. The demon had recovered!

Shit!

I ran fast, putting on his much speed as I could, but it wasn't enough. The sword slammed into the ground, and the shockwave sent Michelle and I sailing. I yelped as my shoulder was ripped from its socket when I struck the hard ground. Rolling across the stone, I only stopped when my back slammed into something hard. Groaning, I climbed to my feet and tried to pretend my back didn't feel like it was broken as I looked around.

It didn't take long to find Michelle. She was lying several yards from me. However, Asmodeus had also seen her. His enraged crimson eyes locked onto the archangel, and a vicious snarl split his face as he raised his sword and brought it down. I tried to move, but even as I scrambled over to Michelle, I knew I wouldn't make it in time.

Just as I was about to scream, Adina darted over to Michelle, picked her up, and took to the skies. The sword crashed against the floor seconds later. Stone was upheaved and flew through the air in chunks as another shockwave ripped across the ground. I stopped running and covered my face, grunting as several large stone projectiles slammed into my arms, legs, and torso. I was lucky I had armor on. I was pretty sure those makeshift projectiles would have pierced right through me if I wasn't.

"You little gnats are beginning to annoy me! You're like a bunch of flies and ants moving about!" Asmodeus roared as he tried to track Adina. However, Vyra appeared in front of his face and unleashed several fireballs that detonated against his eyes. The man roared in anger as Vyra darted away.

Adina landed next to me and set Michelle on her feet. The woman still looked woozy, so I stabilized her with a hand to her back. While she was recovering, Christine raced over to us.

"Are you three okay?"

"I think so," I answered her.

"Good." Christine breathed a sigh of relief before her eyes hardened. "Listen, I'm sure you've realized it, but Asmodeus is way out of our league right now."

"Trust me, I've realized it," I said.

"It's kinda hard not to," Adina added.

"Right." Christine nodded. "However, we can't leave either. Brad and Elric have already tried opening the door out of here, so it looks like our only way to survive this is to defeat Asmodeus."

As we spoke, Brad and Elric were darting around Asmodeus's legs, attacking him in tandem. Their attacks didn't seem to do much. That hard armored skin of his was nigh impenetrable. Even Elric's holy attacks didn't do much damage. His level simply wasn't high enough to crack that armor…

Armor?

"Do you know if there's a way to attack him through that armor?" I asked.

"Maybe." Christine looked over at Asmodeus as he tried to crush Brad and Elric beneath his feet. Vyra, however, kept that from happening by shooting more fireballs at his face. While they didn't do any damage, they did distract and blind him. "I don't really think we can attack through his armor, but if you look closely, his armor has several areas around the joints that are vulnerable."

I looked harder and noticed that she was right. The area around his knees, elbows, wrists, armpits, shoulders, and neck were all lacking in armor, which meant they were the most vulnerable spots we could attack. However…

"Even if we attack his flesh, Asmodeus is still strong enough to shrug off all but the most powerful attacks," Michelle said. "I have already hit him with my second strongest attack, and it did very little damage despite being one of the weakest points of his body."

"What about your strongest attack?" asked Adina.

Michelle shrugged. "It is possible my attack will hurt him, but I highly doubt it will be strong enough to finish him off—and that is what we need, an attack that will finish this demon in a single blow."

I wondered if any of us had that, but I didn't think we did. My strongest attack right now was Triple Thrust. It had a +610 attack power and dealt critical damage. Even so, it wasn't a very strong attack compared to Michelle's Holy Lightning, which had already proven only partially effective against this demon.

"What if we all attacked the same spot?" asked Adina, scratching her head. "Maybe a concentrated barrage to the same area over and over will be enough to take him out?"

Christine, Michelle, and I stared at the woman as she gave us what might have been the most brilliant idea ever.

"Adina, you are either the most brilliant genius in the entire Rift Plains or an incredibly lucky idiot," Michelle said.

Adina narrowed her eyes. "I might not be the sharpest succubus in this lair, but I at least know when I'm being insulted."

"I'm glad you can recognize a backhanded compliment when you hear one."

"So mean."

As Adina and Michelle traded their by now typical banter, I turned to Christine, who was watching the pair like she didn't know what to make of them. I understood her. Here we were, in the middle of a battle against a powerful demon boss, and they were bantering. However, there were far more important matters to think about.

"Christine, can you boost our attack power?" I asked.

"Of course," Christine said, turning away from the sight of Adina and Michelle quarreling.

"Then do it," I ordered. "Boost our attack power as much as you can, as many times as you can."

"That's going to leave me exhausted…" Christine grimaced. "But I'll do it. What's a little exhaustion compared to making it out of this alive."

Christine began glowing a bright orange before she sent her powers into the three of us. I immediately felt my muscles being strengthened. It was hard to describe such a feeling, but if I had to, I'd say it was like when you had to take enhancement steroids after suffering from a severe injury during a mission. It gave me a temporary boost of strength, which could allow even grievously injured soldiers to keep going.

The moment she finished boosting us, Christine dropped to her hands and knees, breathing heavily through her mouth. Her shoulders heaved. Sweat poured from her body. Her face was now pale as though the blood had drained from it. I guess boosting us like this really did require a lot of power.

I would have to thank her later.

"All right." I unsheathed my sword. "Let's do this."

"I'll go first!" Adina volunteered as she blasted off the ground.

"Silly girl! Wait for us!" Michelle shouted as she also flapped her wings and soared through the skies.

I groaned as I was once again left behind, but I didn't complain as I put on an incredible burst of speed. With Christine's buffing spell racing through me, I was able to catch up with Adina and

Swordsman of the Rift

Michelle, who soared through the sky. We were practically neck and neck as I ran along the ground and they the air, though maybe I was a little behind them. Whatever. I could work with this. I'd still make sure I was the first one to attack.

Brad and Elric were already on their last legs, it looked like. Brad's armor was dented and his shoulder pauldrons were missing. Elric was leaning on his mace as he stood on bended knee. He looked almost like a knight kneeling before a queen, save the blood running down his face. His left eye was also squinted shut and blood was running down it.

Asmodeus, the impossibly tall demon, really did resemble a goliath. I already knew that. However, it hadn't really struck me, like in the face struck me, until this very moment. He was so freaking big that I really had to wonder how there could be a space large enough to fit him. Where the hell were we inside of this dungeon? How far down had we gone? I tried to put those thoughts out of my mind as I raced past Brad and Elric and prepared to launch my attack.

Despite claiming I would be the first one to attack, I was not, in fact, the first person who got an attack off. That honor belonged to Adina. She flew straight toward Asmodeus like a bullet, her body corkscrewing around before she slammed her heel into Asmodeus's unprotected knee. Death Kick was an attack so powerful it had a chance of one-shotting an enemy whose level was the same or lower than hers. I'd seen her kick off a demon's head before.

As her foot struck the knee, an explosive bang echoed around the room. Asmodeus roared as his knee undulated. It was like a strange reverberation spread out from inside of his knee, or like the bones inside had been turned into mulch.

Adina leapt away from Asmodeus as the giant's knee wobbled. Before he could fall or do anything else, I had leapt up and attacked the exact same spot. Triple Thrust. I impaled Asmodeus's knee exactly three times, and blood spurted from the wound each time, puncturing a deeper and deeper hole into his knee. More howling echoed from Asmodeus as I leapt back onto the ground.

And that's when Michelle performed her finisher.

I had no idea what to call his attack, but Michelle held her hands out in front of her, and floating between them was a tiny sphere of crackling golden energy. Even from a distance, I could tell how potent this attack was. A shiver crawled up my spine.

And then she threw it.

I don't think I will ever forget the sight. The golden sphere slammed into Asmodeus's knee, which was already greatly weakened, and tore straight through it. I remember watching a show once where a guy's leg got chopped off by a hacksaw. This was a thousand times more gruesome. Her attack tore apart Asmodeus's knee, busting his kneecap apart and shredding everything else to bits. Flesh, muscle, and bones was sliced utterly destroyed. His calf went flying through the air and landed on the ground with a loud rumble. Meanwhile, Asmodeus screamed in agony and rage as he crashed to the ground.

The earth shook from Asmodeus's crash, and I nearly lost my footing because his fall actually caused something of an earthquake. Asmodeus landed on his back. His hands went to his stump of a leg as he roared out his frustration for everyone to hear.

"Gaaa! Gaaaa... fuck you! You cursed angel bitch!" Spittle flew from Asmodeus's mouth as he snarled at Michelle, who landed on the ground beside me and Adina. **"Mark my words, you little fucking cunt! I don't care how long it takes! One of these days, I will find you again, and when I do, I will tear your body apart! I'll fuck you so hard your body will split in half! You will regret ever standing against me!"**

As the man swore and threatened Michelle with enough vitriol to fill an Olympic swimming pool, a swirling vortex appeared behind him. I realized only after he dragged himself into it that what had appeared was actually a portal. Did that mean Asmodeus could create portals?!

"He's getting away!" Michelle shouted in shock.

"Damn it! Don't run away!" Adina snapped. "Release my mother!"

However, Asmodeus either didn't hear her or wasn't listening. Once he dragged himself into the portal, the swirling vortex closed around him, and Asmodeus disappeared.

After Asmodeus vanished through the portal, Brad set himself up as the master of this world. I wasn't sure what he did. It didn't look like anything had changed to me, but Brad assured me this world was now ours. I had shrugged his words off. Without knowing exactly what he was doing, I found myself not really caring.

We were still located in the deepest part of the dungeon where we fought Asmodeus. The stale air was beginning to get to me, but I didn't complain as all of us prepared to move out. We would have to make our way back outside and get to a portal that would take us to the Rift Plains. For a long trek like that, we all wanted to be well-rested, so we were recuperating to regain our strength.

As I sat down on the hard stone floor with Michelle on my left, I found my gaze wandering to Adina. She was floating high above us, hovering around the crystal that her mother was imprisoned in. She had her hand pressed against the glass and it looked like there might be tears in her eyes. I wanted to go over to her, but I couldn't fly.

"If you want to talk to her, I can carry you up there," Michelle suggested when she saw who I was looking at.

"Will you?" I asked.

"Of course." Michelle wore a warm smile as she stood up. "After all, you two are my lovers."

Michelle hooked her arms around my waist from behind and flapped her wings. We lifted off the ground and flew over to Adina, who remained silent as we approached. Her eyes hadn't left the figure inside of the crystal. Adina's mother was completely visible. It looked like her eyes were open with a look of surprise. I could only assume Naamah, the other two succubus, and Asmodeus had caught her in a surprise attack.

"When my mom was sealed, Naamah, Agrat Bat Mahlat, and Eisheth Zenunim joined forces with Asmodeus and launched a surprise attack on her. She didn't even have time to really fight back before they sealed her inside of this crystal." Adina clenched her hands into fists as tears welled up in her eyes. "After that, Naamah took me prisoner and forced me to become her slave. I had no choice but to do the bidding of that woman… and I hated every moment of it."

"You don't have to do her bidding anymore," I said.

"I know." Adina wiped at her eyes to rid herself of the tears before they could fall. "I have you to thank for that, but now I have to defeat the other two, Agrat Bat Mahlat and Eisheth Zenunim." She placed her hands on the crystal's surface. "This crystal is powered by the three succubus queens and Asmodeus. In order to free my mother, I have to defeat the remaining two and Asmodeus. Only when their power is no longer present will the seal on this crystal shatter."

"So it looks like we have two goals," Michelle said. "Figure out what is happening up in Heaven, and free your mother from this prison."

Adina looked at the two of us with startled eyes. "You two are going to help me?"

"Of course we are," I said. "Aren't we your lovers?"

Adina still seemed shocked, but the surprise didn't last long before she broke out in a warm smile.

"Yeah, you are. Thank you."

After our conversation, Adina came back down to the ground with us. We were just in time too. Once we were standing on solid ground, Brad informed us that we were leaving.

We made the long trek out of the dark underground labyrinth. There were only a few monsters hanging around, and we killed these stragglers before they could run away. Most of the demons who made this place their home had already fled through a portal. Only a few had been unable to.

Eventually reaching the area where we had fought against Naamah, our group followed Brad as he let us through a section of the dungeon that was different from the one we originally took when our group first came to this world. It wasn't long before a massive wooden door sitting on steel hinges loomed over us. The door was quite heavy. Elric, Brad, and Vyra needed to use all their strength to push it open.

The path beyond the door was a winding dirt road. I glanced up at the crimson sky, which had rolling thunder clouds hovering above us. This desolate wasteland of a place truly looked like a world of death.

We moved quickly through this wasteland in which nothing lived, and eventually came upon a swirling vortex. All of us walked through it. I blinked several times when I found myself standing in an unfamiliar fortress. The stone walls, floor, and ceiling reminded me of an ancient castle, like something you'd expect to see in medieval Europe. Brad and the others were already walking outside of the fortress, so I followed them with Adina and Michelle by my side.

Outside of the fortress was an unfamiliar forest. I still recognized this as the forest we walked through to get to the vortex that took us to that other world, but it looked like this was a different section, or perhaps it was a different forest within the Rift Plains.

"I plan to station some guards around this fortress later, but that's something for me to do after I get some other matters settled," Brad said as he turned to us. "Now that we've all returned, I believe it's time to log out. Well, I guess we could have done that after taking the fortress. Anyway, see you all on the other side."

I watched as Brad's avatar flickered and vanished.

"Well, this has been fun, but I'm heading out too," Elric said as he turned to Adina and Michelle. "It was lovely meeting you two beauties."

"The feeling isn't necessarily mutual," Michelle said.

Elric just laughed as he turned to me. "See you in a bit, Bryan."

With that, he disappeared as well. That left just Vyra and Christine. Vyra didn't say anything as she vanished from sight, meaning Christine, Adina, Michelle, and I were the only people left.

As we stood there, Adina frowned at me. "You are coming back, right?"

"I am," I confirmed. "I just need to find a portal that will take me to the Rift Plains again." I glanced at Christine. "Isn't that right?"

"It is." Christine confirmed with a nod. "However, finding a portal in our world that will take you to the Rift Plains isn't easy unless you have someone who can guide you to one."

"Would you be able to help with that?" I asked.

"I can, and I will." Christine smiled. "I'll give you the location of several portals that I know of based on your current location on Earth. Where do you live?"

I told Christine what state I lived in and even the city, which caused her to nod and inform me of where I could find a portal. It seemed there were quite a few, more than I expected at any rate, but they weren't anywhere close to me. The nearest one would take a few hours' worth of travel to reach.

"Okay. Thanks for telling me about those portals," I said.

"It's no trouble." Christine waved off my thanks with a grin.

I smiled back before turning to look at Adina and Michelle, the two women who had become my lovers. They were staring at me with pensive frowns. I could tell they were reluctant to part, so I moved forward and pulled them both into a hug. My actions seemed to startle them, but then they were returning my hug, wrapping their arms around me. I relished in the feeling before pulling back.

"Will you two wait here for me?" I asked.

"We will," Michelle said. "We'll stay right in this spot, so you had better hurry up and come back—with your real body this time."

"I want to fuck you in your real body," Adina added. I could tell she wasn't joking. The succubus looked on the verge of crying, which I found somewhat amusing for some reason, though I didn't say anything.

I chuckled at their words before logging out. The last thing I saw of the three women was Adina looking ready to cry and Michelle comforting the other woman. Then the world went dark, I thought I heard a loud whirring noise, and I opened my eyes to find myself staring at a black screen, which took me aback for a moment before I remembered that I had placed one of those VR helmets over my head. I reached up and removed the helmet, revealing the barren warehouse that Brad, myself, and the others had been inside before the start of this mission.

The others were already awake and standing up. I removed my gloves, took off the boots, and discarded my suit.

We had finally returned to our original world. We had returned to Earth.

Adina sat on the ground in the forest, her legs curled into her chest as she leaned her back against a tree. The scent of fresh earth and flowers filled her nose. Colorful green leaves and brown bark gave the area around her a vibrant, lush aesthetic. It was a truly beautiful sight, one that she wished she could enjoy.

Sitting beside her was Michelle, the archangel and her friend. She found it weird that she was friends with an archangel. Yet after everything they had been through together, maybe it wasn't so surprising. They had fought together, slept together, eaten together, and even shared a man together. Adina felt an affinity for this woman with her pure white wings and beautifully pale skin.

They weren't alone. Christine was with them. The woman who had joined up with their group later was admiring some flowers a distance away, giving the two of them a bit of privacy.

"How long do you think we will have to wait?" asked Adina. She didn't need to elaborate.

"I do not know." Michelle sighed and shifted so her legs were spread out in front of her. She placed her hands on her lap and leaned her head back. "I suppose it depends on how long it takes Bryan to get back here."

"I hope he comes back soon." Adina looked at the grass beneath her feet. She had taken off her boots so she could feel the grass. Small blades of soft green tickled her toes as she wiggled them.

"I do as well," Michelle said, smiling slightly. "I have never felt this way about someone before, and I probably won't say this very many times, but I really do love that man."

"Me too."

Adina thought about her life before Bryan had shown up, of the bleakness that had existed in her life. She had lived hopelessly from one day to the next. As a succubus who possessed the lowest level among her peers, she had been abused by just about everyone. Maliperum hadn't even been the worst among her abusers. She was just Adina's handler.

Her life had changed drastically after Bryan appeared. He created a plan that freed her from Maliperum's control, helped her level up so she could content with her enemies, and fought against and killed Naamah alongside her. She was in a better place now because of the things he had done.

"It will probably take him a day to get back," Christine told them as she wandered over to where they were sitting. The blonde human bombshell squatted next to them and grinned. "Sorry for interrupting. I just overheard your conversation and wanted to let you know. According to where he lives back on Earth, the nearest portal to the Rift Plains is about twenty-four hours away if he drove there. He'll probably take a bus or railway to get there, so we can assume it will take an entire day."

"So we have to wait a whole day?" Adina grimaced. "That doesn't sound fun at all."

Christine's bright eyes stared into Adina's as she placed her hands on her cheeks. "So tell me… just how did an angel and a succubus become Bryan's lovers? I'm really curious."

While Michelle flushed pink at being called out, Adina didn't feel the least bit embarrassed as she regaled Christine with how they met Bryan. She told them about his capture, about how she and Michelle had taken care of his injuries, about their escape and how they killed Maliperum, and of course, she talked about their first time having sex. In fact, Adina was certain she talked more about the sex than she had anything else, despite how their single night together had just been a small footnote in their journey.

What could she say? She was a succubus through and through.

"That sounds lovely," Christine sighed, her half-lidded eyes giving her an erotic appearance. "I'm really curious about this Bryan now. Do you mind if I join you three?"

"No," Michelle said.

"I don't mind at all!" Adina said at the same time.

Michelle looked at her. "Adina, I am willing to share Bryan with you because of everything that happened between us, but I do not want to share him with some random woman we only know because she was with his previous teammates."

"But wouldn't it be more fun if she did join us?" Adina said. "Think of all the kinky things we could do with another woman!"

"I-I don't particularly care about such things."

"You're blushing."

"I am not!"

Christine sat on her butt as Adina and Michelle argued. There was no heat in their argument. At the very least, Adina did not feel any ill-will toward Michelle. She actually enjoyed arguing with this woman, who was straight-laced and honest to a fault; it was fun.

Hours passed by, and Adina eventually fell asleep without realizing it. She woke up with her head nestled on Michelle's right boob. Blinking several times, she wiped the drool from her mouth and looked around. It was dark now. She hadn't known the Rift Plains could get dark. For a moment, she wondered what had woken her up, but then a loud gurgling alerted her to the fact that she was hungry.

"Ugh… but we don't have any food," Adina mumbled.

She wondered if she could find some food, but before the idea could really take hold, the loud snapping of branches alerted her to something coming this way. Adina quickly shook Michelle awake and scrambled to her feet. The other woman reacted more slowly than her, but she eventually heard the sound and stood up as well.

Christine, who'd been sleeping on her other side, hit the ground with a thud when he pillow disappeared.

"What the—!" the orange-tinted woman squawked.

Just as Michelle was turning toward the source, Adina saw someone step out from the treeline and into the moonlight. His strong jawline and straight nose were complimented by pale blue eyes and sandy hair. He had a strong physique, powerful arms, broad shoulders, and a thick chest. He didn't have on the armor she'd seen last time. Instead he was wearing jeans and a white T-shirt. However, even without the armor, she recognized his face.

"Bryan!"

Adina didn't know if Michelle had called his name or if she had, but she was running toward the man before he could even greet them. She pounced. There was a loud "Oof!" from Bryan as she bodily tackled him to the ground. Before he could even regain his senses, she was pressing their lips together, penetrating his tongue with her mouth. His taste was a lot stronger now. The taste of cinnamon and coffee was heavy on his mouth. She wondered if that was because he was not an avatar but here in his real body, but the thought only lasted for a second before she shrugged it off and went back to orally ravishing him.

"Get off him, Adina! Allow Bryan a chance to breathe!"

She squawked as Michelle grabbed her by the wings and yanked her off Bryan. She would have complained, but then she saw Bryan looking incredibly dazed and realized she might have gone overboard. He sat up, wincing, then looked at her with a pained smile.

"You really... need to be more careful." He placed a hand against his chest and rubbed it. "This body of mine isn't my level 69 avatar. My real body is only at level one."

"I'm sorry," Adina said as she rubbed the back of her head.

Michelle huffed at her before helping Bryan stand to his feet.

"I'm glad you have returned," Michelle said. "We have been waiting for you." She glanced at Adina. "This one kept complaining about how much she missed you."

Rather than get embarrassed, Adina puffed out her chest with pride. "I am a loyal succubus who couldn't wait to see her man again."

Bryan and Michelle chortled, but then Bryan turned to the archangel and asked, "And you? Did you miss me?"

Michelle flushed. "Well... yes, I did. W-we are lovers, after all."

As the three of them reunited, Christine stood up and walked over to them. She brushed the dust and grass off her clothes and stopped in front of the trio.

"Welcome back, Bryan."

"It's good to be back."

"Now that you are back, we should decide what to do next," Michelle said.

"I want to rescue my mother," Adina added.

Michelle frowned. "We should go to Heaven and see if the rebellion is still ongoing or if someone won."

"Your rebellion can wait. My mother has been sealed inside of that crystal for too long."

"The rebellion in Heaven is a serious matter that should be resolved. I cannot just abandon God or my people."

"Um..." Bryan raised his hand, interrupting their conversation. "I don't know if you guys remember, but I just said I'm only at level 1 right now. That means I'm no longer strong enough to help either of you yet. I propose we find a world where I can level up. We can decide what to do once I'm at a suitable level where I won't hold either of you back."

Adina looked at Michelle, who looked back at her, and through their eyes, a conversation took place.

"Let's go with Bryan's idea," Michelle said at last.

"That sounds like a good idea to me," Adina agreed.

Of course, even though they had agreed to help Bryan level up, it wasn't like they knew which worlds they should go to. Adina had never been outside of Hell. Her original home was the Second Hell, and then she had traveled to the First Hell after her mom was sealed away. While Michelle was a bit more knowledgeable, her knowledge only extended to Heaven, and that was the last place they wanted to go for grinding levels.

Fortunately, there was someone among them who could help out.

"If that is your plan, then why don't you three come with me?" Christine suggested. "I have been traveling through the Rift Plains for over a year now and know of several great worlds that can be used for grinding and gaining experience."

Bryan looked at Adina, who nodded, and then at Michelle, who also nodded. He turned his attention to Christine.

"I think we'll take you up on that," he said.

"In that case, you three, just follow me."

As Christine began walking off, Adina and Michelle came up on either side of Bryan and grabbed his hands. Together, they followed after the human Rift traveler and began their next adventure.

~Fin

AFTERWORD

Hello everyone! It's Brandon Varnell here. I'm glad you all could join me as I attempt to write something I have never done before in my entire life. No, it's not harem. That's almost all I write. I'm talking about gamelit.

Gamelit or LitRPG is a genre I've never touched before. Certainly, I have read a few stories with RPG elements like Is It Wrong to Try to Pick Up Girls in a Dungeon, Log Horizon, and Sword Art Online, but this is the first time I have ever written something like this myself. I'm honestly not sure how well I did.

Because I don't know the western gamelit market that well, I decided to do a lot of research into what other authors were doing. I mostly read audiobooks because they are easier to consume. I bought stuff from authors like Jaime Hawke, William D. Aarand/Randi Darren, Michael Scott-Earle, Prax Ventor, and others. I wanted to know what other authors were doing and what made them successful before attempting to write something myself.

Despite all my research, I still don't know how well I did.

Since I don't know how good this story is, or whether or not I should continue, I thought I'd leave this matter to my readers. If you enjoyed this story, please consider leaving a review to let me know. It doesn't need to be big. Simply writing a single sentence review like: *"This was a fun story!"* would suffice to let me know whether I should continue. If enough people say they like it, I can probably see about turning this into a duology or maybe even a trilogy.

Before I head off, I would like to thank several people. Lonwa_A, my artist, thank you for doing such a great job with the cover art. My editor and proofreaders, thank you so much for help find those errors in my manuscript for me. And you, my readers, thank you so much for reading this story. I can only do what I do because you support me. I'd be living in my mother's basement if it wasn't for you.

At least, I would if my mother had a basement.

Anyway, thank you all again! I hope you'll join me on my next story!

~Brandon Varnell

SNEAK PEAK! WEIDERGEBURT: LEGEND OF THE REINCARNATED WARRIOR

The Ending is Only the Beginning

The air burst all around me. Despite the fact that I was currently a being composed of lightning at that moment, I felt an indescribable pain that forced me to revert back into flesh and blood as my concentration slipped. Flames seared the hair off my arms and caused my skin to crack and burn. Blood seeped from my skin, looking almost like lava leaking from cracks in the earth's crust.

Though I quickly circulated my Spiritual Power, channeling the water element through my body to heal my wounds, I did not allow myself to sigh in relief. More explosions were detonating all around me, forcing me to swerve in every direction. What's more, by channeling the water element and using it to heal myself, I had been forced to split my attention two ways.

The lightning covering my body had grown weaker as a result of my split attention. In that moment, seven figures appeared above me. I glared up at the winged beasts flying over my head. They were naught but shadows. However, those shadows were currently surrounded by intense Spiritual Auras that crashed into me like tidal waves rolling over a small village.

One of those great beasts released an avian cry before it swooped down, and the moment it did, the blazing heat surrounding my body grew even more fierce. Sweat broke out on my skin. It quickly dried up under this unfathomable heat. I could feel my skin getting singed once more, and I knew that I could no longer afford to run.

Since this creature was using fire, I decided to use water.

Dissipating the lightning in my body, I took a deep breath, and then circulated my Spiritual Power again. Instead of the sensation of static crawling across my skin, something soft and almost gel like covered my body. One step further. Grimacing as the heat from the creature closing in caused steam to rise from my body, I channeled more Spiritual Power into myself and transformed my entire body into water.

The great beast was finally upon me. What had appeared was an avian of such immense size that even the dragons living in the Misty Mountain Range could not compare to it. Wings of orange and red fire flapped, causing heat waves to distort the air. Colorful designs ran along its body. It was a mixture of red, orange, yellow, and blue. Its plumage was a brilliant white that burned like an illuminating flame. Red and yellow tails trailed behind it as though simulating the ends of a shooting star. Intense crimson eyes glared at me with a hatred that I knew was mutual.

Gnashing my teeth together, I turned around, tucked my fist into my torso, and put as much Spiritual Power as I dared into my next attack.

The beast drew near. I waited until the last second. Then I quickly spun around, dodging the beast by a hair's breadth. It was so close that my body, currently composed entirely of water, was beginning to boil. Steam rose off my body as the water creating me evaporated. However, I did not let myself get distracted. Thrusting out my fist, I channeled my Spiritual Power through it and created a massive spike of water that extended from my arm.

Even though the intense heat from the flames surrounding this creature was immense, I was no weakling myself. Water evaporated and created waves of billowing steam. Even so, the spear held firm, refusing to dissipate as I encapsulated it with my Spiritual Power, and it soon penetrated the beast's chest. Rather than spewing blood, what emerged from the creature was a bright white flame.

As the beast cried in pain, I immediately retracted myself and prepared to attack again.

That was when one of the other beasts swooped down. I saw the shadow and sensed the intent to kill me and quickly moved away. Once I had reached what I deemed a safe distance from the firebird, I released my control over water and transformed into lightning again. Everything around me immediately slowed up, though I knew this was just my perception of time dilating as the synapse in my brain accelerated to the speed of light. With my newfound power, I was able to safely jump several dozen meters in less time than it took to blink.

The bird that had swooped past me was just as massive as the firebird, but instead of being coated in flames, this one had green and white feathers. Its soft feathers gave it a very gentle appearance. However, I knew from the thousands of razor sharp cuts I'd received during my earlier engagement that I couldn't underestimate its deceptively soft appearance. A long tail moved behind it like a tassel. If I looked closely, I could see the atmosphere around it being cut by thousands of wind blades.

A loud crash caused me to cast my gaze toward the ground. Flames spewed from the ground down below as the fire bird crashed into the forest. I felt a sense of grim satisfaction as the creature shrieked in agony. Brilliant white flames, the lifeblood of that great beast, were spewing from its chest like a fountain.

I did not have much time to admire my handiwork, for the green bird released a sharp cry before charging at me. Knowing that my element was weak against this creature that could control the wind, I used Flash Step Version 3: Lightning Step to move away as quickly as I could, but the beast remained stuck on my tail, creating a vacuum that cut through the atmosphere to increase its speed.

Frowning, I once more split my attention. I didn't do much this time. Channeling the light element into my finger, I took careful aim and sent a condensed beam of light at the wind bird. What I got in return was a satisfied shriek as my attack sheared through one of its wings. Light wasn't strong against wind, but it wasn't weak either. Greenish white blood spewed from the area where the limb had been severed. Without both wings, it was unable to maintain flight and fell to the ground below.

However, just like before, I was given no time to celebrate my success. Five other birds had just descended. Each one was just as big as the previous two. Each one possessed the ability to control a different element to perfection.

All of them had reached the zenith, the Fourth State of Spiritualism, just as I had with my two main elements.

A powerful beam of light slammed into me without mercy, burning my back as it sent me sailing toward the ground. My scream was lost to the wind. My body felt like it was being thrown into the Sun. Everything hurt. But I did my best to shunt aside the pain, increased the flow of lightning through my body, and rolled out from underneath the powerful beam of light.

The beam continued on. It struck the side of a mountain several kilometers below. An explosion so massive that the wind buffeted me despite its distance went up, sending plumes of smoke and rubble into the sky. When the attack died down, the mountain was gone. In its place was a crater so large I was sure it would be visible even if I moved beyond this planet's atmosphere. I grimaced when I noticed how the entire ground inside the crater and several hundred meters out had been turned into glass.

"Damn…"

I looked at the result of that attack, and then turned back to glare at the beast who'd caused it. The massive bird flapped its wings as it glared back. This creature looked like it was made of pure light, a combination of white and yellow feathers that appeared both soft and translucent. Yellow eyes glowed with a power that seemed almost divine.

While the bird and I entered a glaring contest, an intense killing intent slammed into me, forcing me to swerve from the spot where I'd been floating.

Six spheres made of water flew past the spot where I'd been. They slammed into the ground far below. Each sphere created a crater that easily spanned ten or fifteen meters across. Earth cracked. Fissures appeared as trees were felled. It was absolute devestation.

I could not admire the damage this attack did, for the moment I dodged it, I was forced to move again. This time, seven blades of darkness cut through the air. They were nothing more than black ripples that caused space to distort. I swerved over one of them, and then flew down to avoid another. Twisting my body, I managed to avoid two more, but the last one had been aimed at where I would be rather than where I was.

"HA!"

Channeling light into my palm, I slammed it into the blade of darkness, causing the air around me to crackle as arcs of light and dark Spiritual Power raced across the sky. Gritting my teeth as the dark blade pushed me back, I released a furious cry and poured even more Spiritual Power into my palm. The dark blade exploded as I finally tore through it.

The creature that had released this was a bird made from darkness so pure it was like a black hole. Sharp wings covered its body. The only part of it that wasn't black were its eyes, which were pure white and contained no pupils. Alongside it was a bird with blue feathers, one with yellow feathers, another with brown feathers, and the light bird that had attacked me earlier.

I took a heavy breath as sweat poured from my brow. However, I knew I couldn't stop. Without even trying to recover, I released the restraints on my Spiritual Power, and then I began absorbing the surrounding elements. I drew water molecules from the air and used them to bolster my strength.

The friction generated from energy leaping from small molecules was also absorbed into my skin and increased my Spiritual Power. My body became energized as though the last several hours had never happened. I could feel the Spiritual Power coursing through me like a tempest. Light mixed with water and lightning inside of me, some of which leaked out because my body simply couldn't withstand the power output.

"Dammit… I had been hoping to save this for your boss," I muttered in a bitter voice.

Whether or not the five elemental birds heard me, they certainly knew that my threat level had suddenly increased. All five of them screeched as they gathered their own Spiritual Power. It congealed around their mouths, forming spheres of condensed energy. Barely a second had passed before they launched their attacks. Five beams of water, lightning, light, darkness, and earth flew toward me.

I did not meet their attacks head on. I wasn't stupid.

Using the power of light, I immediately vanished from the spot where I'd been standing. Their attack went through my after image. I didn't give them a chance to be surprised. Reappearing several meters above the most troublesome of the five, I turned myself into a streak of light and descended before it realized what I was doing. I barely felt any resistance as my body blew a whole clean through the black bird.

Landing on the ground at almost the exact same instant I had moved from the point above the darkness elemental bird, I looked up to see that my attack had done what I intended. The black bird with powers over darkness now had a large hole in its chest. What's more, the edges were frayed flesh refused to heal. While darkness was the antithesis of light, the same was equally true.

"Kari, I still have no real grasp over your affinity, but it is only thanks to you that this was possible," I said to myself as I watched the massive bird slowly break into particles of darkness.

My attack enraged the four remaining birds, who quickly descended toward me. I didn't even need to use Spiritual Perception to feel their intent to kill me. Almost before I could even move, they had each launched their own attack. The four elements of water, light, lightning, and earth swirled around each other to create a mixed beam of power so large it could engulf a small city.

But I was no longer there.

As their attacks slammed into the forest floor and caused even more damage to the environment, I was already in front of the water bird. I reached out with my hand and touched its head. The bird's eyes were crossed as it stared at me, but I just smiled at it. I'm sure my smile was quite cold.

The water bird lit up as I shoved as much lightning into it as I could. Even though the water composing its body was quite pure and couldn't generate electricity, I could use my own water element to force impurities through its body. My lightning then ran rampant through it. With a shriek so loud it was nearly inaudible, the bird lit up like fireworks during the Summer Solstice. Smoke soon rose from its body. However, it was too slow. This attack could definitely kill it, but the other birds would get to me first.

Clicking my tongue, I raised my hand, which had turned into a five meter blade of lightning, and then I brought it down. My attack created a seam of light within the bird, a small line that appeared from its beak to its tail feathers. The bird peeled apart at the seam, the two halves almost gently falling away from each other before the elemental beast turned into water that rained upon the ground.

Barely a second had past before something sharp pierced my back. I couldn't even cry out in pain as the air was stolen from my lungs. The ground beneath and the sky above blurred past me in dull streaks. Gritting my teeth, I turned my head and found the enraged eyes of the light bird glaring at me. It had pierced my back with its beak.

"Don't think…" I struggled to raise my hand. "Don't think…" Light, lightning, and water swirled around my arm as I channeled all three elements. "Don't think this will be enough to do me in!!!"

With a roar of defiance, I crashed my fist into the light bird's beak. A loud cracking sound echoed from the beak as an incision line appeared. One incision became two, then two became three, four, eight, sixteen. It quickly multiplied before cracking underneath the power of my fist.

The bird immediately stopped flying as it thrashed and screeched in pain. However, the forward momentum it had generated was enough that I was not able to stop flying until I generated enough force with my own Spiritual Power to stop myself.

Reaching behind my back after I had stopped moving, I pulled out what remained of the beak from my back and tossed it away. Warm blood spilled down my flesh. I ignored it as I eyed the three remaining elemental birds. The lightning bird, the wind bird, and the now injured light bird.

"Ha… ha… ha…"

My shoulders heaved as I glared at the birds. However, I didn't think my glare was very effective just then. The Spiritual Power flowing through me was fluctuating. The aura covering my body flickered in and out. I didn't reveal my thoughts, but I was swearing up a storm internally as my Spiritual Power started running dry.

This technique I was using wasn't complete yet. What's more, it was hard to absorb the natural elements when I was using more than one at the same time. If I'd had time to finish it, then maybe I could have already ended this battle, but it wasn't like I could have waited until I was ready—not after Erica told me about what happened while I was gone.

It looked like the birds were just about to renew their attack, and I myself was prepared to re-initiate hostilities, but all of us suddenly froze in place as an intense Spiritual

Pressure filled the air. My breathing quickly grew heavier as sweat formed on my brow. It was a cold sweat. I tried to take in a breath, but the pressure was causing my lungs to struggle with the simple act of taking in oxygen. It felt like something was crushing them.

A figure had suddenly appeared in front of me. He was a luminous being more beautiful than the Sun, a creature of such incomparable beauty that even in my hatred, I could not deny there was not a single flaw to be found. Pure white robes covered his body. Long and silver hair flowed freely like a waterfall down his head all the way to his bare feet. His long, pointed ears were the clearest signs that he wasn't human.

He did not have a very muscular body. Indeed, I would have said his body was quite feminine. He was slender and willowy. However, I didn't let that fool me, and even if he had been a woman, I wouldn't have underestimated him like some people would have done.

Despite his beauty, there was something odd about this man. Every part of him seemed bright and divine—every part except his blood red eyes. They were a dark crimson that seemed tainted somehow. Furthermore, that dark aura surrounding him seemed to present a direct contradiction to his vibrant, almost divine appearance.

The man took a deep breath as he looked at the three birds. He surveyed them with a slight frown, and then quickly glanced at where I had killed the others. I wanted to move, to attack this man with everything I had, but some invisible force kept me in place. Even if I attacked now, I wouldn't be able to land a good hit.

Finally, he looked at me.

"To think a half-blood like you was able to defeat four of my seven slaves," he murmured. **"You know I had enslaved these monsters specifically to kill you? Your powers are indeed great. Given enough time, you might even pose a threat to me. It seems trying to send enslaved**

Demon Beasts after you was a mistake. I should have just come myself."

"Great Overlord of the Seventh Plane…" My fists shook with barely restrained hatred as I stared at the being before me. "You took everything from me. My wife. My child. Everything. I have waited for this day, waited for the day I would finally face you again, for the day I would finally kill you."

The being before me, the one I called the Great Overlord of the Seventh Plane, chuckled as though I had said something amusing. It was a grating laugh, not at all like something I'd expect from such a feminine figure. His laugh caused the hair on my neck to prickle.

"Had your wife not shielded you from me, she would not have died. She only has herself to blame." He paused, his head tilting as he stared impassively into my rage filled eyes. **"As for your daughter… I could not allow a human who possesses such divine blood to live. Had I not killed her, she would have become a threat."**

"A threat?" I whispered. "We were just living peacefully when you attacked us unprovoked and without warning. We were no threat to you. You laid waste to our home, destroyed our civilization, and killed my family without even a hint of mercy or provocation."

The Great Overlord of the Seventh Plane snorted. **"You may not understand it now, but you are indeed a grave threat to me—no, you are perhaps the greatest threat to ever exist. What I did was necessary."**

I didn't think the blood flowing through my veins could have run any colder than it already was, but I was wrong. It was like my blood had frozen over. Only a chilling coldness that seeped through my entire being remained.

"Necessary, you say?"

"Yes. Necessary."

"Necessary… for what?"

"To keep you from being able to interfere with my plans." The Great Overlord of the Seventh Plane spread his arms wide and chuckled again. **"Just look at what you have done. A half-blood who hasn't even learned to control even a tenth of his abilities has defeated four of my seven slaves, Divine-rank Demon Beasts capable of annihilating entire cities with a single attack, and you would have defeated all of them had I not intervened. I'd say this level of destruction warrants intervention."**

I had no idea what this monster was talking about, but I was done listening. He had attacked my family for a reason as dumb as protecting himself? From what? It was true that I had been the one who awakened him, but I had never harmed him nor had any intention to. Had he never appeared attacked my city, never attempted to kill me, never murdered my daughter and wife, we would have left him alone.

My hatred surged, allowing me to overcome the intense pressure that had been pushing down on me. I compressed the last remaining Spiritual Power in my body. The aura that had been covering me vanished. To the average eye, it would have looked like my power had disappeared. I didn't even turn into an element this time.

The Great Overlord of the Seventh Plane narrowed his eyes.

Then I vanished.

It happened in a flash. I appeared directly behind my foe, thrusting out my fist in a punch that caused the air to burst. However, without even looking behind him, the Great Overlord of the Seventh Plane placed his hand in the direction of my punch, catching it. A shockwave erupted from the contact.

I was already moving.

Appearing on his left in a manner that was almost like teleportation, I launched a powerful kick. This was also blocked. I was undeterred. I appeared again and again, moving all around him at speeds so fast I left multiple afterimages in my wake. One. Two. Four. Sixteen. Thirty-four. Sixty-eight. One hundred thirty-six punches were delivered in less than a second. Yet no matter how many punches and kicks I threw, no matter how fast I pushed myself, this monster blocked each and every one of them as though it was easier than breathing.

Meanwhile, I was running on empty.

With the last of my strength, I released a vicious scream and channeled all my energy into my fist. A bright glow erupted from it. The air around it distorted. Ripples spread through the sky as though the fabrics of reality itself were being torn apart.

The Great Overlord's eyes finally widened. With something resembling panic, he threw out his own punch, which glowed in the same manner as mine but with a dark energy that seemed vile and repulsive. The air exploded between us as one fought to overpower the other. I gritted my teeth and pushed as hard as I could, wrecking my body. Blood exploded from my arms as my capillaries burst, my muscles tore apart like they were made of soggy parchment, and I could feel my very life being drained.

I didn't care. It didn't matter if I died so long as I killed this man.

Perhaps it was because I was so focused that I didn't see the attack coming at me until it was too late. However, when a fist appeared out of nowhere, all I could do was swear. The attack hit me. Pain overrode my ability to see, causing a white film to cover my eyes.

I think I must have passed out. When I came to, I was lying on my back, in the middle of a massive crater so large I couldn't even judge its size. The Great Overlord of the Seventh Plane was above me, a sword made of pure darkness grasped firmly within his right hand. He raised the sword and brought it down.

In a last ditch effort, I unleashed all of the Spiritual Power I had left, channeled it into my right hand, and met the blade with a punch. Our attacks struck each other. Light bent. Air warped. Lightning crackled. It wasn't enough. More. I needed more. Gritting my teeth, I gathered all the elements under my command. Light streaked in and enhanced me. Water motes wirled around my hand. I even absorbed the lightning from the divine lightning beast and used it to fuel my attack. With a snarl, I compressed all of these elements together.

The Great Overlord of the Seventh Plane gasped. The area around our mutual attacks became distorted as strange cracks appeared in the atmosphere like the gaping maw to a bottomless abyss. An explosion suddenly rent the air as the world around me was torn apart. The last thing I saw before darkness engulfed me was the Great Overlord's surprised crimson eyes.

Hey, did you know?
Brandon Varnell has started a Patreon
You can get all kinds of awesome exclusives
Like:

1. The chance to read his stories before anyone else!
2. Free ebooks!
3. exclusive SFW and NSFW artwork!
4. Signed paperback copies!
5. His undying love!
Er... maybe we don't want that last one, but the rest is pretty cool, right?

To get this awesome exlusive conent go to:
https://www.patreon.com/BrandonVarnell
and sigh up today!

A
Most
Unlikely
Hero

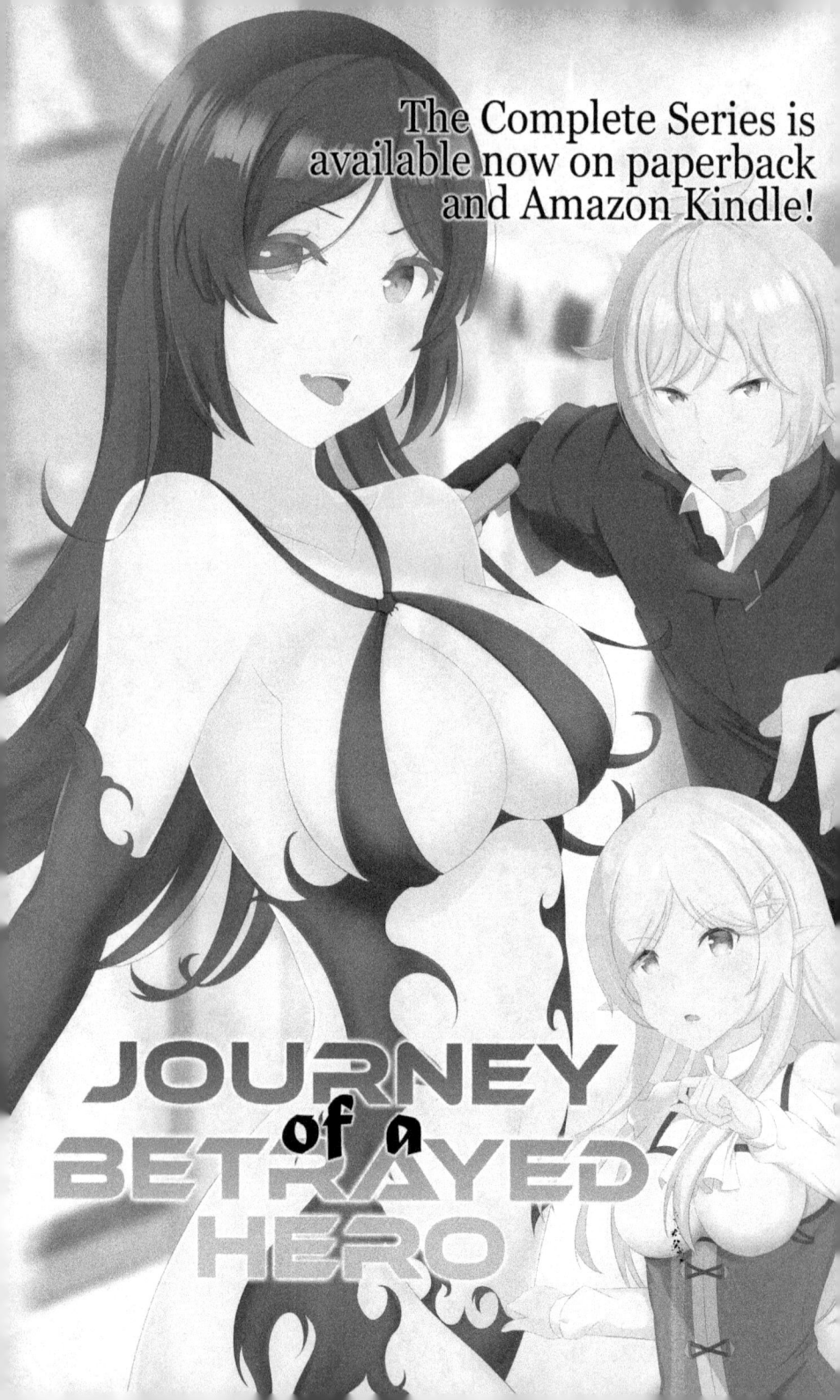

The Complete Series is available now on paperback and Amazon Kindle!

JOURNEY of a BETRAYED HERO

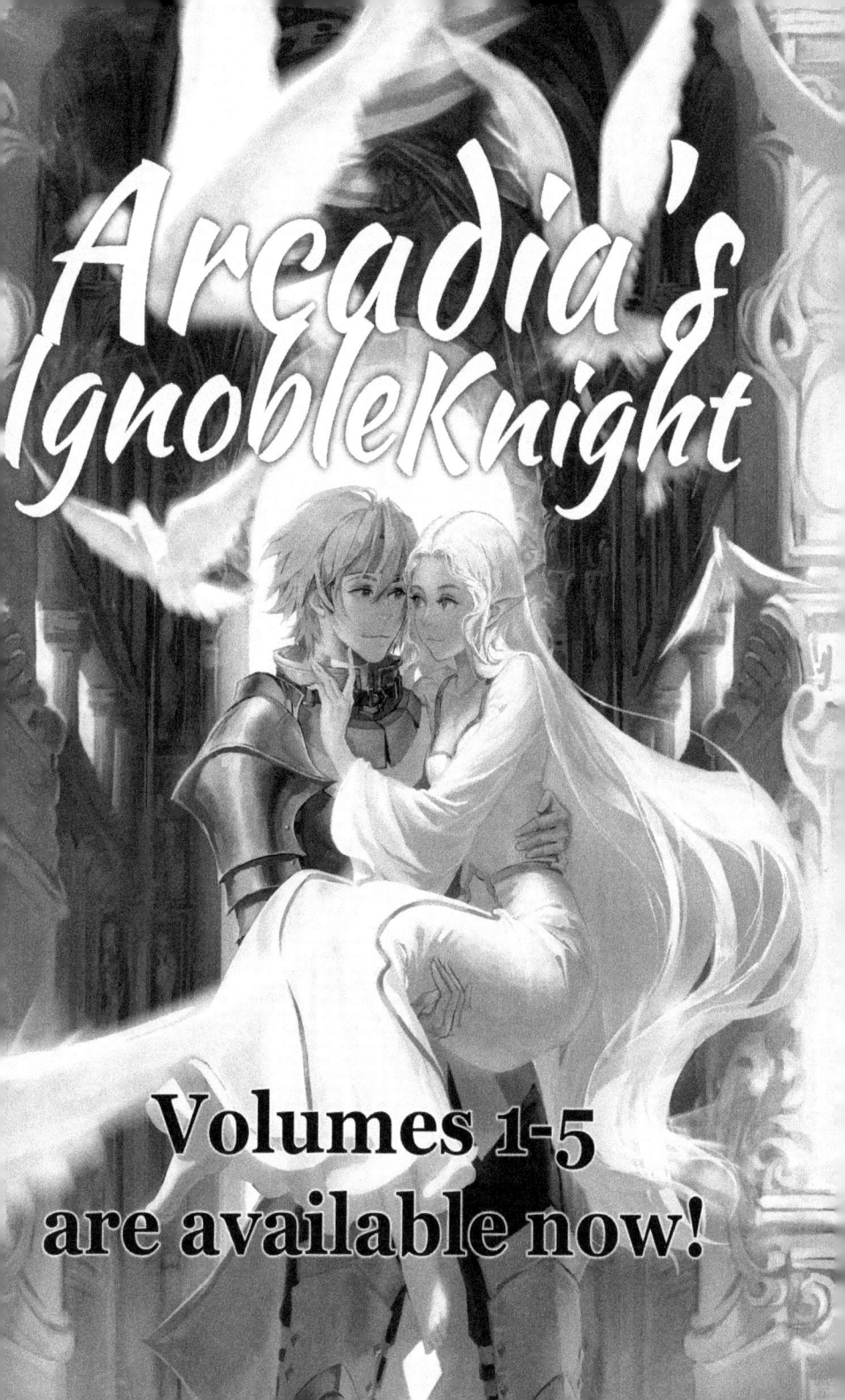

Want to learn when a new book comes out?

Follow me on Social Media!

 @AmericanKitsune

 +BrandonVarnell

 @BrandonBVarnell

 http://bvarnell1101.tumblr.com/

 Brandon Varnell

 BrandonbVarnell

 https://www.patreon.com/
BrandonVarnell

www.ingramcontent.com/pod-product-compliance
Lightning Source LLC
Chambersburg PA
CBHW061034120726
47910CB00006B/2251